TESSA CAVENDISH IS GETTING MARRIED

SUZIE TULLETT

BLOODHOUND
— BOOKS —

www.bloodhoundbooks.com

Print ISBN 978-1-5040-7257-1

For every quirky mother out there
Long may your enthusiasm continue

I lay in the bath, marinating in water that had long since cooled. I knew I should get out before my lips turned blue, but with every passing shiver I told myself just one more minute. My stomach rumbled as the mouth-watering aroma of Leo's cooking drifted up into the room. Despite feeling hungry I resisted its lure. Everyone knew how snappy and uncooperative I could be when I had an empty belly, and plying me with food was, no doubt, an exercise in damage limitation. A means for Leo to minimise any scene I might cause.

Leo had been acting strange for days. Ever since his visit to see his brother, Nial, up in Cumbria, he'd been nervous and on edge; nothing like the laid-back guy I knew and loved. I'd asked him what was wrong because he clearly had something on his mind, only to be met with dismissals and smiles that never quite reached his eyes. I thought I'd go mad if I heard him say *I'm fine* one more time. We'd been a couple long enough for me to know when he was lying, and recognising all the signs, I had a good idea why. He was getting ready for the *it's not you, it's me* speech.

As much as it hurt, I had to admit our break-up was inevitable. Leo, the tall, dark and handsome party-lover, was always going to get bored of a plain, but scrubs-up-well-if-pushed, homebird like me. In our thirties, we might be similar in age but personality wise, we couldn't be more different. While his weekend away had been a chance to catch up with his equally outgoing brother and friends, it had enabled him to get out and have some fun for a change, obviously making him realise what he'd been missing.

I scoffed. No wonder the man had taken to spending night after night teaching the dog new tricks, as if getting Otis to balance a treat on his nose was more entertaining than anything I had to offer. *Otis.* I would miss that dog too. He and Leo came as a package, and I'd got used to having both of them around. I scolded myself for believing that Leo was in our relationship for the long haul. No matter what people said opposites didn't really attract.

"Dinner's almost ready!" he called up.

I frowned as I mimicked Leo's words. *Dinner's almost ready!* I knew I was being childish, but I couldn't help myself. Usually keen to sample the man's gastronomic delights, as far as I was concerned that night's dish could burn. Continuing to avoid the unavoidable, I stayed right where I was.

I sighed. It was okay for Leo. He could scurry back to Cumbria and get on with his life. I, on the other hand, had no choice but to face the fallout. It wouldn't just be me losing myself in ice cream and break-up songs, my whole family would be seeking solace. The Cavendishes hadn't only welcomed Leo with open arms, they'd fallen for the man, and telling them Leo and I were no longer a couple was not going to be easy. Mum would be the worst. No matter the issue, she always came down on Leo's side. I could already picture her disappointment and hear what she'd insist were words of wisdom.

"Don't say I didn't warn you. Cooping yourself up in that shed of yours Monday to Friday, spending your weekends in front of the telly." Whenever Mum described my life, she always tended to oversimplify. The numerous hours I spent reading, dog walking, or with a sketchpad and pencil never got a mention, while the *shed*, as she liked to call it, was, in fact, a pottery studio. "A man like that was bound to get bored. As for what you look like…"

I ran my hand through my wet, half-curly, half-straight mop of hair, while my eyes settled on the old jeans and sweater that sat crumpled in a pile on the bathroom floor.

"…a bit of a tidy up once in while wouldn't go amiss."

It was not a conversation I looked forward to.

Dismissing thoughts of my mother altogether, I inhaled a huge gulp of air, held my breath, and sank my whole body under the water. I listened to my heartbeat reverberating in my eardrums; a sound I found strangely comforting and womb-like. Concentrating on the rhythmic *d-dum, d-dum, d-dum*, I tried to empty my mind of woes.

A shadow cast over me and my eyes flashed open as someone grabbed my shoulders and yanked me up from the water. Panic-stricken, my pulse quickened, and arms flailing I attempted to defend myself, until, finally, my assailant let go.

"Jesus, Tess, what the hell are you doing?" The colour had drained from Leo's face and his shirt was soaked. Standing there, he stared at me horrified, while I stared back gasping for air.

"What the hell are *you* doing?" I asked, coughing and spluttering. I sucked much-needed oxygen into my lungs and waited for my breathing to settle. "Because if you're trying to give me a heart attack you almost succeeded."

"I shouted up, but you didn't answer."

"I was seeing how long I could hold my breath for." Putting on a brave face, no way was I admitting to self-pity.

"I thought you'd drowned." Leo plonked himself on the edge of the bath. He dropped his head into his hands for a moment, before returning his attention to me. "I thought you were dead."

My eyes widened. "And I thought I was being murdered."

Leo took a deep breath and exhaled, before standing up again.

He picked up my bath towel and opened it out for me to step into. "Time to get out of there, I think. Don't you?"

I looked at my shrivelled, deathly pale skin and knowing he was right, hauled myself out of the water. I let him wrap the towel around me for what felt like the last time, closing my eyes as he kissed my forehead and squeezed me in his strong embrace. Resting my face against his chest, I could have stood there forever. Unlike Leo, I soon realised, who, after a few short seconds, was happy to let go.

"I'll see you downstairs, yeah?" he said, turning to leave. He paused in the doorway and as he gave me a final glance, I struggled to interpret his expression. "You're one strange cookie, Tess Cavendish. You know that?"

Watching him disappear, a wave of sadness washed over me. I wished I could say that we'd fallen out; argued over something to the point of no return. At least then I'd have understood his strange behaviour and neither of us would be walking on eggshells.

Drying myself down, I realised it was time we were both put out of our misery.

CHAPTER 2

*H*eading downstairs, I wore my favourite flannelette pyjamas. If I was going to be an emotional wreck, I wanted to make sure I was at least physically comfortable. Having assumed he would be in the kitchen putting the finishing touches to our last supper, I was surprised to see Leo sat on the bottom step waiting for me. Then again, after the bathroom incident even I'd lost my appetite and as I imagined us both sat at the table forcing food down our necks, it felt consoling to know it was a meal neither of us looked forward to.

I slowed in my movements to observe him. Despite what he was about to do, my heart went out to Leo. Hunched forward, he rested his elbows on his knees and his chin in his hands. With his back to me, I couldn't see his face, but I could picture his forlorn expression. Breaking up with someone was never easy and I knew he'd be hurting as much as I was.

Despite my tiptoeing, a stair creaked to announce my descent. Leo thrust his hands behind his back as he rose to face me and while I wondered what he was hiding, he gave me another of his forced smiles. Appearing as anxious as I felt, he swallowed hard as I approached. "Put this on," he said, suddenly extending one of his arms my way.

I stared at the blindfold in his hand recalling how Leo had just deigned to call me strange. "Why?" I asked, suspicious.

"Because I want you to."

I eyed the length of black cloth. Unless Leo was about to dump me by standing me in front of a firing squad, blindfolds symbolised a surprise celebration, not an ending. *Oh, Lordy.* As I took in Leo's eager expression, I asked myself how I could have been so stupid. Wanting to take back every negative thought I'd had about the man, I didn't know whether to laugh or cry. If only I could figure out what we were meant to be commemorating. Although in that moment, we could have been rejoicing the arrival of spring, such was my relief.

"Tess, are you okay?" Leo asked.

I let out a whimper and grabbed the banister to steady myself. "Yes and no," I replied, my voice suddenly three octaves higher. I hastily stepped forward and throwing my arms around him, hugged Leo tight. As I breathed in the scent of his aftershave, I felt his body relax and his arms envelop me. Enjoying the moment, I couldn't believe all the misery I'd put myself through.

I suddenly pulled back. "Stay where you are." Leaving him stood there, I calmly headed down the hall and into the kitchen. Letting myself out into the garden, I paused for a moment, before finally allowing my emotions to burst forth. I jumped up and down and squealed in delight, not caring that I looked like a complete idiot as I launched myself into a range of happy dances. Being wrong had never felt so right.

Finally I stopped, and Floss, Carlton, and Moonwalk over with, I took a second to centre myself, ready for events to continue. Re-entering the house and making my way back down the hall, I repositioned myself at the foot of the stairs and took a deep breath. "You were saying?"

While a part of me was overwhelmed with happiness, another part felt mortified. On the one hand, Leo hadn't been working up to the *It's not you, it's me* speech at all. On the other, when it came to dates and special occasions, I had a memory like a sieve. Wracking my brains, I knew it couldn't have been Leo's birthday. Not only wouldn't there be a blindfold involved if it had, in my small circle of family and friends, such celebrations were like proverbial buses. They all came at once. To say the back end of the year was an expensive time was an understatement. With Christmas on top, my bank account took a hammering.

Of course none of that made me feel any less guilty. While Leo had secretly made plans to mark some special occasion, I hadn't only failed to mention it, I didn't even know what it was. No wonder Leo had been distant; he was probably disappointed in me. In his position, I'd have been the same.

I sneaked a glance towards the lounge, hoping to spot balloons or a banner that might give me a clue, but the old oak door was firmly shut. "It's our anniversary, isn't it?" I said, tentative. "Of the day we met?"

Leo chuckled, enough to tell me I'd guessed wrong.

I didn't mind him laughing at me. It was the first genuine smile I'd seen on Leo's face since he got back from Cumbria. I wrinkled my nose and took another stab. "Of the day you moved in?"

Still the man said nothing.

My shoulders slumped. Whatever I'd forgotten, it was clearly important. "Come on, Leo. Help me out here." I was beginning to feel desperate.

He indicated the blindfold. "Not until you cover your eyes."

"But you know I don't like surprises."

Leo refused to give in.

Observing his determination, it was clear I had little choice in the matter. Not that I was in any position to argue. We'd have been there all night if I'd had to work it out. "Okay," I said, my shoulders slumping. "If I must."

Leo tied the blindfold around my head, before fiddling with the fabric at the front to make sure I couldn't see. "You ready?"

"As I'll ever be." With my world suddenly black, I felt Leo take my hand and as he guided me the few steps to the lounge, butterflies fluttered in my tummy. Opening the door to let us in, I felt the warmth of the open fire and heard the crackling of logs. He steered me to the couch and lowered me into a seating position.

"No peeking," he said.

As he let go of me completely, I sensed him step back. I heard shuffling and then Leo whispering something. "What's going on?" I asked. "Who else is here?" Curious as to who Leo was talking to, I suddenly felt self-conscious. If I'd known we had company, I'd have foregone the flannelette.

"You can take it off now," Leo said.

Untying the blindfold, I had to blink to clear my vision. At last able to focus, my breath caught, and I put a hand up to my mouth. A smile spread across my face at the sight of Otis sitting patient and still. "So that's what the dog treats were about," I said. I gaped at the ring that balanced on the black Labrador's nose – a gold band, home to a huge solitaire diamond. My look fell on the neckerchief he wore, which bore the words *Will you marry my daddy?* Tears threatened my eyes as I turned my attention to Leo.

Crouched on one knee, he looked nervous. "Well?" he said. "Will you?"

I struggled to get my head around what was happening. Moments before, it was as if I'd been plummeting down the steepest of tracks bracing myself for a crash landing into singledom; only to suddenly find myself racing skywards again. As my regard flitted from Leo to Otis to Leo, I couldn't imagine a proposal more romantic. My tears began to fall, and my heart swelled. I nodded. "Yes," I said, my voice barely audible.

Leo's face broke into a smile, before he jumped to his feet and pulled me up into an embrace. Planting his lips firmly on mine, he lifted me into the air and spun me round. Dropping me back down onto terra firma, he produced a treat from his pocket and turning to Otis, gave him a fuss before swapping the ring for the dog biscuit.

I smiled with glee as Leo took my hand.

"You sure about this?" he said.

Again, I nodded, and I couldn't help but giggle as he placed the engagement ring on my finger. "So, it's not some anniversary then?"

Leo laughed. "No, it's not."

I held my hand up to the light and took in the glistening diamond.

"It was my grandmother's," Leo said.

"It's beautiful." Having gone from thinking I was about to lose the man in front of me, to knowing I'd be spending the rest of my life with him, I suddenly felt overwhelmed, and a sob escaped my lips.

"Hey." Leo pulled me close. "Don't tell me you're regretting this already."

I laughed through my tears. "Not at all. You've just been so distant lately. Asking me to marry you was the last thing I expected."

"*I've* been distant." Leo looked at me, aghast. "What about you?"

"I thought you'd had such a good time in Cumbria with your brother that you were about to dump me."

"And I thought you'd enjoyed having your own space so much, you wanted to make it a permanent thing." Leo let out a chuckle. "Honestly, I nearly backed out. I really was scared you'd say no."

"So why did you go through with it?"

Leo looked at me, his expression tender yet serious. "Because I knew I'd forever regret it if I didn't."

"I'm sorry. I should never have doubted you. Doubted us."

"I'm sorry too. For making you feel that way."

CHAPTER 3

APRIL

"What's *that?*" The shock on my sister's face was a picture. "Wow!" she said. Grabbing my hand, she looked from my engagement ring to Leo then to me. "Since when?"

We'd just landed at Sal's for the Cavendish family get-together. Taking it in turns, it was my sister's month to play host. I'd meant to take the ring off and keep it hidden until everyone had arrived so Leo and I could make a proper announcement and, having forgotten to do that, I blushed at the sudden attention.

Sal wore a big smile as she threw out her arms. "Congratulations," she said, giving first me, and then Leo, a hug.

Leo put his arm around my waist. "Thank you. Your blessing means a lot."

"Well, I can't deny…" Sal said.

Here we go, I thought. The woman couldn't help herself.

"…that I think you're both mad."

Sal's remark came as no surprise. My sister had never believed in marriage. As far as she was concerned, devoted couples didn't need a piece of paper to prove their commitment in a relationship and while Leo chuckled, I rolled my eyes.

"Don't get me wrong." Sal began busying herself making a pot of tea. "I really am pleased for you both."

"But?" I said.

She paused to look at me like I was from another planet. "Duh. Our Mother!"

Having expected Sal to launch into some speech about marriage being nothing more than a patriarchal institution, I laughed, unable to understand her reasoning.

"You find it funny now," Sal said, as she filled the kettle with water and set it to boil. "But believe me, Mum's been waiting for one of us to tie the knot ever since that Louise Patterson extravaganza."

Louise, an influencer-come-local-celebrity, had had what could only be described as the wedding of the year. Held in an exclusive hotel, Mum had relished every press detail. Apparently, Louise's dress was hand embroidered with pearls and had a ten-foot train. There were wall-to-wall flowers and a six-tiered cake so huge it didn't just have to have its own table, the table had to be reinforced. The champagne bill alone must have cost thousands and I'd have put money on her poor parents still paying for the event. They must have been gutted when the marriage didn't last.

"Our wedding will be nothing like that," I said. Happy in my quiet life, I couldn't imagine anything worse than saying my vows in front of hundreds of people. "We want a small, more intimate, affair."

"Well good luck getting it. Mum's already got a dozen hats and three mother-of-the bride outfits to choose from."

"Don't exaggerate."

Sal raised an eyebrow.

"Honestly," I said. "Mum will be fine."

"Where is everyone, by the way?" Leo asked, glancing around the room.

"Ryan's out collecting dinner." Sal poured the tea and handed out the mugs.

Out of all the Cavendish get-togethers, I enjoyed Sal's the most. Unlike me, who found hosting stressful, and Mum, who preferred a more formal affair, Sal took a relaxed approach to her afternoon. Stuck in the kitchen all week thanks to her cake-making business, the last thing my sister wanted was to slave over the cooker come the weekend.

"And Mum and Dad are running late. Something to do with a rogue parrot in the garden," Sal carried on. "It belongs to one of the neighbours. He's coaxing it down from their tree as we speak."

"And India?" I asked, sipping my tea.

As if on cue, my eleven-year-old-but-acts-like-a-teenager niece entered the room. "Doctor Sanders," she said. "If you don't mind."

I took in her seriousness, along with the white coat she wore, complete with pens poking out from its chest pocket. Her typically unruly blonde hair was scraped back into a neat ponytail and a pair of glass-free, black-framed spectacles balanced on the end of her nose. "Where's your stethoscope?" I asked.

She flashed me a look. "I'm not *that* kind of doctor."

"Really?" I put my cup to my lips and lowered my voice. "Probably for the best with that bedside manner."

"India's toying with the idea of becoming a scientist," Sal said. "She's trying to get a feel for the job before deciding."

"That makes sense," Leo said, giving the girl an encouraging smile. "The *try before you buy* approach."

India's expression softened. "I knew you'd understand." She turned to Sal. "If you need me, I'll be in my room doing science stuff." She got herself a glass of water, turned, and headed back upstairs.

The front door sounded as it opened and closed. "It's only me," Ryan called out. He entered the room laden with brown paper carry bags. "I hope you're all hungry?"

"Starving," I said. "What are we having?"

"Chinese." Ryan plonked the bags of food on the kitchen counter, while Sal grabbed a stack of plates from the cupboard. She handed them straight to me so I could start laying the table.

"What's *that*?" Ryan asked. As I paused in my actions, he nodded to my engagement ring, shock written all over his face.

Sal chuckled as she got together the required cutlery.

"Beautiful, isn't it?" I said. "It belonged to Leo's grandmother."

Ryan's eyes widened further as he took my hand. "That stone's huge." He turned his attention to Leo. "What did your granddad do for a living?"

Sal continued to laugh. "Bet you're glad I don't want one."

"You can say that again. That must have cost a fortune." Ryan smiled. "When did all this happen?" He took the plates I held and put them to one side, before pulling me into a bear hug. "Congratulations, Tess." He turned to Leo, shaking his hand. "You're brave, aren't you? Knowing what these Cavendish sisters are like."

Leo laughed, while Sal grabbed a tea towel and threw it at Ryan. "Watch it," she said.

Ryan turned serious. "Does Patricia know?"

I shook my head. "What is it with you two and Mum?"

"Not yet," Leo said to Ryan. "Although I might have discussed it with Ed."

News to me, I stared at Leo. "When?"

"Before I went to Cumbria."

I cocked my head. I hadn't had the man I was planning to marry down as a traditionalist.

"What can I say? I like to do things properly."

I smiled, picturing the two men. Leo nervously asking for my hand in marriage. My father feeling important for once and loving every minute of it. "Aw, that's so sweet," I said, stretching up to kiss Leo's cheek.

Sal made a vomiting noise. "Someone, hand me a bucket."

"Yoo hoo!" Mum's voice sounded from the hall, signalling her and Dad's arrival.

"Hold on to your hats, guys," my sister said, not even trying to hide her amusement.

"Good luck." Ryan stifled a smile and bit down on his lips.

I shook my head at their childishness. "How old are you two again?"

Mum, with Dad in tow, breezed into the room, as usual wearing perfect hair and make-up, and clothes ironed to within an inch of their life. "Something smells good," she said. Her eyes settled on the foil food containers that Sal carried over to the table. "Oh." Mum's face fell. "Takeout. Again."

"You don't have to eat it if you don't want to," Sal said.

Mum cast her eyes over Sal's granite worktops and snazzy appliances. "I don't know why you bought this kitchen. It's not like you ever use it."

My sister and I smirked, knowing Mum viewed both our career choices in the same way – as hobbies. Growing up, she'd insisted we could be anything we wanted to be, only to suffer disappointment when we took her at her word. Apparently, potter and cake maker didn't have quite the same ring as lawyer and doctor.

"Takeout's fine," Dad replied. He gave Mum a nudge. "Isn't it, Patricia?"

"So how is everyone?" Mum asked. Taking off her coat, she made a point of looking for somewhere to hang it.

Leo smirked my way before stepping forward. "Let me."

Mum sighed dreamily as he disappeared down the hall to

hang it up for her. "Such a gentleman." She pulled herself together. "You don't know how lucky you are, Tess."

Leo made his return, and I couldn't help but smile as he and Dad shared a knowing look. Watching the two men I loved most in the world, a warm glow came over me. "Right, who's for a glass of wine?" I asked.

Sal didn't miss a beat. "Me."

Ryan raised his hand. "And me."

I took a bottle of white from the fridge, while Sal got the glasses.

"Dad, would you like some?"

"Not for me. Driving duties."

"What's *that*?" Mum said. Any higher and her shriek would have shattered glass. "Edward, look!"

Grappling with the corkscrew and wine bottle, I paused.

With her eyes firmly on my left hand, Mum's jaw dropped as her gaze moved from me to Leo. "But that's a…"

Sal leaned into me. "Told you so," she said, her expression smug.

Mum put a hand up to her chest. "When did this happen? I can't believe it." She began struggling to breathe. "Oh, my word. This is wonderful." Her gasps continued.

While Leo and I looked at each other wide-eyed and shocked, Dad pulled out a dining chair for Mum to sit on. "Come on, love," he said. "Calm yourself now."

As Mum plonked herself down, it was clear she was having a happiness-induced panic attack.

"Ryan," Sal said, ready to medically intervene. "Pass us one of those brown paper bags from the Chinese, will you?"

CHAPTER 4

I stirred, not wanting to rouse from the deepest of sleeps. But as I clung on to the most beautiful wedding dream, it was no good; I began to properly awaken. I turned onto my side and smiling, opened my eyes. My smile disappeared. Expecting to see Leo laid next to me, his half of the bed was empty. Disappointed, I rolled onto my back and supposing I should get up too, stretched out in all directions. Rising to a seated position, I swung my legs off the mattress and stuffed my feet into my slippers.

The appetising aroma of Leo's cooking drifted out from the kitchen causing my belly to rumble as I made my way downstairs. "Something smells good," I said, as I entered the room.

Showered and dressed, Leo's hair was still wet as he busied himself at the Aga. Otis sat to attention close by, ready to pounce should there be a spatula mishap. "Great timing," Leo said, as he placed the last of his pancakes onto the mountain he'd already made. "Breakfast is served."

I poured us both a cup of freshly brewed coffee and carried them over to the table that Leo had laid in readiness, while he switched off the heat. Fetching our breakfast with him, Leo joined me and, as Otis took up position between us, I stared at the mound of fluffy deliciousness.

"Tuck in," Leo said.

I didn't need telling twice.

Picking up my knife and fork, I lifted three pancakes onto my plate. Smothering them in maple syrup, I sensed not just Otis's eyes watching my every move, but Leo's too. I paused. "What? Everyone knows breakfast is the most important meal of the day."

"You say that about every meal," Leo said.

The man was right. But I'd always had a good appetite and thankfully for me, no matter the amount of food I put in my mouth I never gained any weight; I maintained a healthy size twelve. I closed my eyes and savoured the taste. "Perfect."

Leo let out a laugh. "You say *that* every mealtime too."

"Have you told your mum and dad yet?" I said. "About the wedding?"

Leo shook his head. "I'm planning to later."

It would've have been nice to inform them in person, but with Grace and Bill living in Ireland that would've meant packing a suitcase and taking a road trip. Apparently, the two of them had always dreamed of living in a little Irish cottage by the ocean, so when, just before Leo and I met, they announced they were upping sticks and moving over, it came as no surprise to Leo or his brother. However, what did come as a surprise was the wreck Grace and Bill had bought. Apparently, Leo's parents weren't renowned for their DIY skills.

"You nervous about it?" I asked.

"Why would I be?"

"Because they might hate the idea. They haven't even met me." We'd been meaning to go over. But as Leo's parents focused on settling into their new life and a mammoth house renovation, day-to-day living eventually got in the way for us too.

"Yes, they have," Leo said, surprised I'd think otherwise.

I stared at the man. "A quick hello into a phone screen is hardly the same thing." While Leo often video called his parents, I found joining in way too awkward and Leo had never pushed me on the matter. I'd say hi to them and that was that. A thought suddenly struck me. "What if your mum reacts like mine?"

Leo laughed. "My mother has her quirks, but I don't think she'll border on passing out."

As I continued to eat, I told myself I was worrying over nothing. Just because Patricia Cavendish was a woman of extremes, that didn't mean Grace was too. "So, what else was on the agenda for today?" I said, moving the conversation on.

Leo's smile grew. "I thought we might start planning the wedding."

Wondering why the haste, I stopped chewing. "She's got to you, hasn't she?"

"Who?"

I couldn't believe he had to ask. "Who do you think?"

Leo chuckled, the image of Mum's happiness-induced panic attack, no doubt, as imprinted on his brain as much as it was on mine.

"I dreamt about it last night," I said.

"About what?"

"Getting married. I don't know where we were. The background was a bit hazy. But it was an outdoor ceremony."

"I like the sound of that."

"The weather was gorgeous. All blue skies and gentle breezes." I came over warm and fuzzy just thinking about it. "I'm guessing it must have been September because there was a definite Indian summer vibe to it. Of course, you looked as handsome as ever in your suit trousers and waistcoat. You wore a tie, but casually. And your shirtsleeves were rolled up to about here." I indicated right below my elbow.

"That's very me."

"I thought so."

Leo laughed again.

"And my dress... You know, I actually felt like a princess." Simple in design, there was no embroidery or fussiness to it. It was tea length and had a skirt that flared in a 1950s fashion. With three quarter sleeves and a neckline shaped into a deep V at the chest, in my mind's eye it was perfect, and I made a mental note to sketch the dress after finishing breakfast, while the image was still fresh. "Oh, and Mum wore the widest of brimmed hats. A turquoise organza affair, all feathers and silk flowers. Completely ridiculous."

"I can't say I'm surprised."

"Even Sal had tears in her eyes, and she doesn't believe in marriage." I stopped eating for a moment. "Everything was perfect." I let out a dreamy sigh. "It was like starring in our very own Hallmark movie."

Leo reached out and squeezed my hand, bringing me back to reality. "Then let's make it happen. Let's do the same."

I looked at him, aghast. "What? Get married in September? *This* September?"

"I don't see why not."

Both pleased and surprised, I'd assumed we'd have a long engagement. I leaned over and kissed Leo's cheek. "I'm up for that if you are?"

Leo grinned. "We better get organising though. It doesn't give us much time."

"You're joking, aren't you?" I said, smiling. "September's months away."

As I dug into my food once more, my excitement began to wane. I slowed in my chewing. Unable to get the picture of my mother breathing into a brown paper bag out of my head, my brow furrowed.

"Everything all right?" Leo asked.

"I can't stop thinking about Mum," I said. "Her response to our engagement wasn't exactly normal, was it?"

"To be fair to her, it did come as a surprise."

"But what if Sal's right? And Mum is expecting a big event? The next few months are going to be a nightmare."

Leo reached out again. "You're worrying over nothing. Patricia's just happy for us."

I sighed, before returning my attention to my breakfast. "Maybe. But I still think we need to tread carefully."

"Yoo hoo!"

I froze, my fork coming to a sudden stop halfway to my mouth. Frowning, I looked at Leo. "You were saying?"

Leo shook his head and smiled. "Trust me. She'll be fine."

CHAPTER 5

*M*um glided into the room, pausing to take a good look at me and Leo. Beaming, she exuded happiness. "And how are you two lovebirds this morning?"

"All the better for seeing you," Leo replied.

While my husband-to-be took Mum's arrival in his stride, I eyed the woman, suspicious. Mum didn't usually turn up at someone's house uninvited. She considered not giving advance warning bad form, even when it came to visiting her daughters.

"Coffee?" Leo asked, already out of his seat.

I watched Mum glance over at the kitchen worktop. If she thought my sister's kitchen was too pristine, she held the opposite view when it came to my cluttered and somewhat eclectic space. From the pre-loved wooden dresser heaving with an array of mismatched crockery, to the hanging pot rack that teemed with well-used pans, to the old ceramic farmhouse sink… my little abode was the stuff of Mum's nightmares. Twitching at the mess that Leo's cooking had left, she was obviously weighing up whether she should risk it.

"Yes, please," Mum replied, her voice suddenly strained.

I crammed another forkful of pancake into my mouth just as

Leo whipped my plate away. My shoulders dropped as I watched him scrape my breakfast into Otis's bowl, while the dog's tail wagged in frantic anticipation. As soon as his bowl hit the floor, Otis dived straight in.

"I came to apologise." Mum took a seat at the table. "For my reaction the other day."

Leo placed her cup in front of her, while I narrowed my eyes. As genuine as the woman appeared, saying sorry was something else Mum never did.

"No apology necessary," Leo said. "It's great that you're so happy for us. Isn't it, Tess?"

"Mmm," I said, not yet ready to commit one way or the other.

"Still. I did go a bit overboard," Mum said.

Talk about an understatement. "We all know how much you love a good wedding," I said.

"Oh, I do," Mum replied. "But it's not only that. I'm just so pleased for you both, I can't tell you."

I took in Mum's smile, unable to deny her sincerity.

"You two getting married is the most exciting thing to happen to this family in years. Apart from the usual birthdays and Christmases, the last time we had real cause for celebration was when India was born."

Recalling Mum's pure joy at becoming a grandmother, I felt humbled. Mum had never been the warm and fuzzy type and the thought of her experiencing the same degree of delight over mine and Leo's engagement was heart-warming. A pang of remorse hit me for all the moaning I'd done about the woman.

"And I'm here to help in any way I can. You do know that, don't you?"

"Thanks, Mum," I said.

Mum looked from me to Leo, her eyebrows raised in anticipation. "All you have to do is say."

Despite Mum's heart being in the right place, I couldn't

believe she expected a job list there and then. "Well, we've not really decided on any details yet. Have we, Leo?"

"But it'll be good to have you on hand when we do," he said to Mum. "We haven't a clue where to start."

I watched Mum's eagerness turn to glee and realising we still needed to be cautious I looked to Leo. As he opened his mouth to continue, I stared at the man, wide-eyed, willing him to please shut up. However, telepathy clearly wasn't my strong point.

"It's not like either of us have done this before, is it, Tess?" he said.

Mum put a hand to her chest. "I'm so pleased you've said that." She jumped from her seat. "Because I've put together some ideas." She hastily headed out of the room.

"What happened to us treading carefully?" I asked Leo, keeping my voice low. "How could you not see she was looking for an in?"

"Tess, she's your mum. It's only natural that she wants to be involved."

"Involved I can cope with. It's the takeover bid that worries me."

Leo chuckled, yet again failing to share my concern.

"I'm telling you, she won't be able to help herself."

Mum reappeared with a huge A1 art folder and an even bigger smile. Unzipping her wares, she pulled out a huge collage made up of magazine cut-outs, fabric samples and colour charts.

Dumbfounded, I stared at her handiwork. "You've put together a mood board?" I couldn't believe what I was seeing, unlike Leo, who looked impressed.

"It's just a little something to get you started."

Little was not the word I'd have used.

I took in the numerous images before me – pictures of ice sculptures, humongous wedding cakes, and brides wearing white feathered capes. Mum had even stuck fronds of fir and eucalyptus to the ensemble. She obviously had a winter wedding in mind. "Is that a photo of Saint George's Chapel?" I asked, hoping against all hope that I was wrong. "Surely you're not suggesting we get married at Windsor Castle?"

"If it's good enough for royalty."

Desperate for his assistance, I again turned to Leo. However, he appeared as enthralled with the images as my mother was. "Mum, you do know that not just anybody can get married there, don't you?" I said.

"Why not?" Mum asked, suddenly serious.

Mortified by the question, I found myself lost for words.

At last, her face broke into another smile. "Don't worry. I'm only teasing. It's merely an example of what to look for in a venue."

"You think we should hire a castle for our wedding?" Her explanation did nothing to ease my concerns. "Mum, we don't have that kind of budget." I indicated her creation. "And even if we did, I'm sorry, but this isn't what we want." A part of me felt bad for dismissing her efforts, while another part realised Sal had been right in her warning. Needing to take control of the situation, I knew I had to stay firm. "We're aiming for a quieter, more relaxed affair. Something small." I trained my eyes on Leo. "Aren't we?"

"Define small," he and Mum said.

As I looked at them both, aghast, it was clear I was on my own. "Anyway, we haven't even pinned down a date yet," I carried on.

Leo turned to me, puzzled. "But I thought..."

I glowered his way and the man fell silent. "So, all this Winter Wonderland stuff..." I continued, again waving a hand in the board's direction. "...may not be appropriate."

"I thought you might say that," Mum said.

"You did?" I replied.

"But don't worry, I'm one step ahead of you."

Watching her reach down for her art folder, unlike Leo who

sat to attention, I whimpered when Mum proudly pulled out three more boards.

"I've done one for every season." She looked back at me, proudly. "See?"

I swallowed hard. Struggling to conjure the right words, I stared from one collage to the next and the next and the next. Spring, Summer, Autumn, and Winter, they were all there. Each offering as detailed and as extravagant as the other.

CHAPTER 6

*W*ith Mum gone, and Leo and I having broken the news of our engagement to Grace and Bill, I'd pinged a message to my friends Abbey and Chloe suggesting a group call so I could tell them too.

The three of us had been close since our first day at university and while we each went on to live miles apart, Abbey in Scotland, Chloe in Cornwall, and me in the Yorkshire Dales, even years later we kept in regular contact. It came as no surprise to find my phone lighting up almost immediately thanks to an incoming video call and as I settled myself on the sofa, I smiled when their eager faces popped up on my screen.

I took in Abbey's bright red hair. "Look at you." Abbey was forever playing around with her appearance, which was always as colourful as her personality. I shook my head. Last time we chatted she'd been blonde.

"Very cool," Chloe said, acknowledging the change too. She let out a sigh. "I can't remember the last time I got to a salon."

Chloe was more like me when it came to personal styling. Whereas I lacked interest, her approach to fashion was borne out of necessity. As the mother of a three-year-old, Chloe didn't have the time nor inclination to think beyond the practical.

"What I'd do for a bit of pampering right now."

"Ruby keeping you busy?" I asked.

Chloe let out a laugh. "And then some."

"So, come on," Abbey said. "What's the big announcement?" It was just like her to get straight to the point.

I smiled as I raised my left hand and wriggled my fingers in front of the camera.

Abbey and Chloe squealed and bounced up and down at the sight of my engagement ring.

"When did this happen?" Chloe asked.

"Have you set a date yet?" Abbey asked.

"Yes, long engagement or short?" Chloe asked before I could reply.

They both looked at me in anticipation.

"Short," I replied. "We've decided on September."

Their eyes widened. "What, *this* September?"

I nodded. "I'll let you know as soon as we have the exact day and time. So you can mark it in your diaries."

"You bet we will," Abbey said.

Chloe fell silent.

"Is there a problem?" I asked.

She took a deep breath. "No. However, you're not the only one with news." She screwed up her face. "Dom and I are having another baby."

"Excuse me?" Abbey and I said. It was clearly the first *either* of us had heard of this.

"I'm pregnant."

"Since when?" Abbey and I said.

Chloe smiled. "Since about two months ago. I haven't mentioned anything before now, because, you know, it's early days. But it's looking like I'm due October time, which means I can be there."

Having thought she'd been about to tell me she couldn't, my relief was palpable.

"Chloe that's fantastic," Abbey said.

"A little brother or sister for Ruby," I said, imagining her as the doting older sibling. "She must be so pleased."

Chloe rolled her eyes. "She'd rather have a puppy."

I laughed.

"Anyway, if you're about to ask me to be bridesmaid." Chloe paused as if reluctant to continue. "I'm gonna have to pass."

My smile froze. Trying to hide my disappointment. I'd been hoping that along with Sal and India, both Abbey and Chloe would be in the wedding party.

"Because if this pregnancy is anything like my first, it's not going to be pretty."

I understood, of course. Thinking back, poor Chloe had had an awful time carrying Ruby. What should have been three months of morning sickness didn't only go on for nine months, there was no let-up; it was twenty-four seven.

"Can you imagine the stress of getting to dress fittings from all the way down here, let alone dealing with on-the-day emergency alterations. Remember first time round, I ballooned in those final couple of months."

The last thing I wanted was for Chloe to feel bad. Bringing a new life into the world was way more important than my wedding service, even if the day wouldn't quite be the same. "Maybe we should change the date? Because bridesmaid or not–"

"You'll do no such thing!" Chloe looked aghast at the mere suggestion. "No matter what happens, I'll be there."

"But should you be travelling come September. What if you go into labour?"

"Don't they have hospitals in Yorkshire?"

I could see she was determined.

"Which brings me to my news," Abbey said, tentative.

Taking in her sudden hesitancy, this was not how I anticipated our call going down.

"You know how I've always talked about opening my own gallery?"

My eyes widened. Having her very own exhibition space had been a dream of Abbey's for years. "You mean..."

"Yes, I've finally found the perfect premises. At least, they will be if all goes as it should."

"Abbey, that's wonderful," Chloe said.

"At last," I said. "I was beginning to think this would never happen."

"It's an old barn on the edge of a popular village. The perfect spot for attracting tourists and locals alike. Currently it's just four walls and a roof, but I've been granted planning permission to put in a second floor." She beamed. "Which means I can use downstairs to sell my work and upstairs as a studio."

"You've already got planning permission?" I asked. "You mean this has been in the pipeline for a while?"

"It came through a couple of days ago. And like Chloe, I didn't want to say anything from the off in case things went awry."

"I'm so pleased for you," I said. "You must be thrilled."

"The builders have been lined up for ages. Finally, they can get stuck in."

"I'm *thrilled* for you," Chloe said.

"The location's great but the building itself is a long way from usable. It needs a tonne of renovations which are going to take months. I'll be project managing, of course."

"Of course," Chloe and I said. We knew Abbey was a control freak when it came to work-related projects.

"Which means–" Abbey said.

"You can't be bridesmaid either?"

She shook her head. "Afraid not."

"You will make the ceremony though, won't you?" I asked. "Because again, we could change–"

"Try stopping me!"

"Is it too early to hat shop?" Chloe asked.

"It's never too early," Abbey said.

Listening to my two friends excitedly chat, I realised it didn't matter that they weren't participating in my wedding. Simply having them there to celebrate with me was more than enough.

"We're also on the end of the phone if you need anything," Chloe said. "If the run-up to your wedding is anything like mine, you're going to need plenty of moral support."

"Plus we want regular updates," Abbey said.

"And vice versa," I replied. "Sounds like this year's going to be full-on for all of us."

"Tell me about it," Chloe said, placing a hand on her belly.

"Bring it on," Abbey said. "It's going to be great."

CHAPTER 7

"You should have seen her, Sal. She was so pleased with herself." It might have been a few days since Mum's visit but that hadn't stopped me imagining the woman sat at her dining table, scissors in hand, ready to tackle the copious wedding magazines, fabric samples, and frills laid out in front of her. I shuddered, yet again shaking the image away. "I felt really bad telling her she'd wasted her time. She'd put so much effort into them."

Neither Leo nor I usually worked weekends, but as a gardener, spring was a busy time for Leo. It was when most people turned their attention to their outdoor spaces, so while he and Otis were out pricing up a job, I'd hoped to spend the day in my studio. At least that had been the plan.

Following Mum's visit with the mood boards, I hadn't been able to concentrate. All week, sitting at the pottery wheel had been a pointless exercise and that Saturday was no different; no matter how I handled it, the clay continued to fold under my hands. In the end, I'd given up and gone round to my sister's, hoping to share my mother-of-the-bride woes.

I stood leaning against the kitchen counter, sipping a mug of tea, while Sal stood on a wooden stool rooting in a floor-to-ceiling larder cupboard, home to row upon row of jars, packets, and bottles. I waited for a few comforting words of wisdom, but my sister continued her search in silence. "Sal, are you even listening to me?" I asked, frowning. I felt like I was talking to myself.

"There you are," Sal said. She smiled a satisfied smile as she retrieved a box of baking powder and a bottle of red food colouring. She stepped back down to floor level. "Sorry. I don't mean to be rude. India's been nagging me for these all morning and I promised to dig them out."

"How is she? Still playing at being a scientist?"

My sister nodded in the direction of the hall. "What do you think?"

India appeared in the doorway wearing a head-to-toe paper forensic suit. Seeing the baking powder and food colouring, her eyes lit up behind her glassless black-framed spectacles. "Finally," she said. Taking both items from her mother's hands, she headed straight out into the garden.

"A thank-you would have been nice," Sal called after her.

I looked at my sister, confused. "What's all that about?"

"She's conducting an experiment."

"What kind of experiment?"

Sal shrugged. "Haven't a clue."

Unable to believe Sal's indifference, I stared at my sister, agog. "Aren't you worried?" For all Sal knew, her daughter could be about to blow up the place.

"Not particularly. There are no dangerous chemicals involved."

I almost spat out my tea. "I should hope not."

I stared out of the window into Sal's garden. It was as stylish as the rest of her house. At the far end was a seating area, paved in rustic slate and with an ultra-modern firepit. A wide pathway followed the whole perimeter line, inside which sat a rectangular lawn. Concrete fenced beds and hardwood troughs, home to various ornamental grasses, palms, and bamboo, gave the garden an architectural feel. Unlike my wildflower oasis, Sal's garden was clean and low maintenance. Exactly how she liked it.

Sal reached for her mug and joining me, we both watched on as India hauled a paddling pool out of the garage and placed it in the centre of the grass. "So, what are you going to do about Mum?" Sal asked.

"Hopefully, I won't have to do anything. Not after talking to her."

Sal looked at me, amused. "Really?"

"What?"

"Let's just say you're not the most direct of people. Unlike me, you tend to be a bit soft when it comes to putting your foot down."

I scoffed. "I consider people's feelings, you mean?"

My sister smiled. "That's one way of putting it."

"In this instance, I couldn't have been any clearer about the kind of wedding we want. Which believe me, is nothing like the one Mum had in mind."

Sal came over all pensive. "Don't you think she has a point though?"

I jolted my head. This from a woman who didn't believe in marriage.

"Assuming you're only going to do this once, why wouldn't you want to go all out? Don't most brides want to be a princess for the day? The ones I've made cakes for seem to."

"Would you?"

"If I was the marrying kind?" Sal thought for a moment. "Probably."

I chuckled, realising there wasn't any *probably* about it. Unlike me, my sister had no problem having all eyes on her. "In my view, most of it's a waste of money," I said. "The important thing is the *I do* part. All the other stuff feels a bit extra."

"And Leo?"

"What about him?"

"Does he feel the same?"

I pondered the question, recalling how Leo's eyes had lit up at the sight of Mum's mood boards. Leo hadn't mentioned that he preferred a big affair, but I couldn't deny he appeared to like the idea. Dismissing my train of thought, I told myself I was being daft and ignoring the knot developing in my stomach, insisted I was worrying over nothing. "He'd have said something if he didn't."

We watched India head back into the garage again, only to reappear with a wheelbarrow loaded to the brim with two-litre fizzy drink bottles.

"Here's hoping Mum got the message then," Sal said.

"I'm keeping everything crossed. She nodded in all the right places. That's got to be something, right?"

India began pouring each bottle's contents into the paddling pool.

"I'd loved to have seen Leo's reaction," Sal said. "He must think she's mad."

"If only. He thinks it's only natural for Mum to be excited."

"Ah, but there's excited and there's excited."

"That's what I said."

Sal laughed. "And then there's our mother."

"Exactly!" Continuing to look out of the window, I shook my head at the situation I was in. "Honestly, the details in those boards, Sal. Anyone would think Leo and I were famous. Then again, even if we were, I still wouldn't want to walk down the aisle with my hands in a muff."

With her cup to her lips, Sal let out a laugh, spraying herself with tea.

I laughed at the mess she'd made. "Or expect guests to drink from a champagne fountain."

"Oh, I don't know," my sister said, her amusement continuing as she mopped herself down. "I'd give that last one a go."

"Maybe I would too at someone else's wedding." I fell quiet for a moment. "It's not funny really, Sal. I dread to think what other ideas Mum's going to come up with."

"You can blame Louise Patterson. It's her fault you're in this mess."

India poured the red food colouring into the mix, giving it a good stir with her hand before picking up an altogether different bottle.

"Is that washing-up liquid?" I asked, watching my niece discharge the whole lot into the paddling pool.

Sal nodded. "Which reminds me, I need to add that to the shopping list." She turned serious. "When you think about it, as much as we blame LP, Mum's always been the same. Remember our school nativity plays?"

I let out a laugh. "Don't remind me." While the other shepherds were wrapped in white tablecloths and wore tea towels on their heads, Mum made sure our costumes were full-on authentic. With our ankle-length robes, attached coats and traditional matching head pieces, we could easily have been extras in a big budget film project. I cringed at the thought. No matter the character, Mum gave our costumes the same attention to detail, and while the teachers might have loved her efforts, for some of the children, they were a source of ridicule. "I think I've still got a shepherd's crook somewhere."

India made her way to the garage yet again, this time returning with a couple of empty buckets in one hand, while dragging a hosepipe along with the other. My curiosity grew as she half-filled the buckets with water. "Now what's she got?" I asked. She seemed to be opening tube after tube of sweets.

"Chewy mints."

"Like Mentos?"

"Yep."

India dropped them into the buckets of water, then added Sal's baking powder.

"I suppose I could ring Mum," I said, getting back to the discussion at hand. "Arrange to nip round just to make sure we *are* all on the same wedding page."

"It wouldn't hurt I suppose. Plus it might put your mind at ease. For all your worrying, she could have listened to your every word and has locked her scissors and glue stick away."

I hoped Sal was right. Mum might have delusions of grandeur from time to time, but deep down I knew she wouldn't really want me to have a wedding day I'd rather forget.

The front door opened and closed. "You'll never guess what Patricia's gone and done!" Ryan suddenly called out.

I closed my eyes, praying it wasn't anything to do with my and Leo's wedding.

CHAPTER 8

"You've got to see this!" Ryan said.

Sal and I spun round as Ryan burst into the room.

"Honestly, you're not going to believe it." He waved a newspaper around, desperate to show us what he'd found.

"Believe what?" Sal asked.

Plonking the paper down in front of us, Ryan eagerly flicked through the pages. "Brace yourselves," he said, struggling to contain his excitement. Finally, he found what he was looking for.

Curious as to what all the fuss was about, Sal and I looked down at the article. My stomach sank. Mum clearly hadn't listened to a word I'd said. "Please tell me this is a joke," I said, desperate.

Ryan chuckled. "You should be so lucky."

"Why is she doing this to me?" Staring at the huge photo of me and Leo, I didn't know which was worse. The fact that we were even there, or the image Mum had chosen to submit. The camera had always loved Leo, but I wasn't so lucky, and I cringed at the thought of my demented smile appearing on every newsstand, phone screen, and breakfast table across town. I thought back to our family gathering and Mum's insistence that we mark the occasion with a few snapshots. If I'd have known Mum was going to run a feature in the local paper, I'd have flat out refused. "Look at the state of me," I said.

Sniggering, Sal put a hand up to cover her mouth, while I wanted to die of embarrassment. "I've seen worse photos of you."

"Now you're being kind."

"It's a full-page notice, telling everyone about your engagement," Ryan said. "There must be a shortage of news this week. Look at all the write-up."

"But why?" I asked, not daring to read the piece. "After everything I said."

"I told you. When it comes to Mum you have to be forceful," Sal said.

Ryan's focus shifted. "What's she doing?" He nodded in his daughter's direction.

"An experiment," Sal said.

"Really?" Ryan asked. "What kind of experiment?"

Watching India pick up her first mix of water, baking soda and mints, and pour it into the paddling pool, Sal and I shrugged. However, Ryan's interest grew, and he wandered outside for a closer look.

We continued to observe through the window as India poured her second bucket's worth into the paddling pool. As soon as the last drop landed, my niece immediately darted out of the way, leaving her dad stood there, evidently as bemused as us by India's sudden haste. Mine and Sal's eyes widened, and our faces lifted skyward as a huge volcano of thick red foam erupted high into the air. "What the...?" we both said. The foam, at last, began to rain down, covering everything in sight. Including Ryan.

"My beautiful garden," Sal said. "It's ruined."

As India hopped and skipped in delight, she turned to give Sal and me a thumbs up.

Ryan continued to stand there red, soapy, and motionless.

Mortified, Sal looked from her daughter to Ryan and back again, while my attention returned to the awful newspaper photo.

"I'm going to kill her," Sal said, of her daughter.

"Me too," I said, of our mum.

CHAPTER 9

$\mathcal{I}$ let myself into our cottage and continuing to fume over Mum's full-page announcement, I marched down the hall and into the kitchen. I plonked my bag and Ryan's newspaper down on the dining table and, without saying a word, headed straight for the fridge. Pulling out a bottle of wine, I handed it to Leo.

In the middle of preparing dinner, he stopped chopping vegetables to open it. "One of those days?" he asked, while I reached in the cupboard for a couple of glasses.

I watched him pour, nodding for him to keep going until I put up a hand for him to stop. Raising the glass to my lips, I downed the lot. "Something like that," I said, ready for a refill. After decanting me a second, more reasonably measured, drink, Leo got back to his task at hand. He tossed Otis a piece of carrot, while I retrieved the newspaper off the table. "You'll never guess what she's done now?" I said. "Honestly, I could murder the woman."

"I take it we're talking about Patricia?"

"Who else?" I turned the pages until I found the offending article. "Look," I said, holding it up.

Leo stopped what he was doing, his eyes widening as he scanned the page. "Is that us?" He wiped his hands on a tea towel and took the paper from me.

"In all our glory."

He chuckled as he read. "She doesn't give up, does she?"

"It would seem not." I drank another mouthful of wine. "I'm going to have to talk to her. Again." I considered my sister's earlier advice. "Sal thinks I should be more forceful with her."

"Maybe. Although I still think she'll calm down at some point." Leo smiled as he took another look at the announcement. "As over the top as this is, you can't deny it's a sweet thing to do."

"Sweet?" I scoffed, unable to believe what I was hearing. "Leo, the woman's gone mad. First those blooming collages, and now this. It's like we've unleashed a monster."

He let out another laugh, leaving me wishing I could share his amusement.

"I'll give her a call," I said. "Arrange to go and see her."

"Do you want me to come with you?"

I shook my head.

"Two against one?" Leo said, one eyebrow raised. "It might make a difference?"

Finally, I felt myself relax. "I appreciate the offer, but when it comes to Mum, you're worse than me. At least I'm trying to put a stop to her. In your eyes the woman can't do any wrong. Besides, there's no point both of us taking time off work." I decided to change the subject. "How did you get on today, by the way?"

"Good actually. They liked my ideas. They especially liked the quote, and they want me to start as soon as possible."

"That's brilliant."

"I still need to thank Ed for recommending me."

"They got your name through Dad?" I asked, surprised.

Leo nodded. "I can't wait to get started. They're a lovely old couple. And if anyone can give us any tips it's them."

"Tips? On what?"

Leo smiled. "After fifty years of wedded bliss, who better to advise on what makes a happy marriage?" He returned his attention to the paper. "This is a great photo."

"Of you, yes." I took the newspaper from him and stared at the image again. "I've ruined some pictures in my time, but this one beats them all. I mean look at me. Have you ever seen such an unnatural smile?"

Leo chuckled, his agreement obvious.

"It's not funny," I said. "If I can't relax for a family snapshot, goodness knows how the wedding photos are going to turn out."

Leo took the paper from my hand and placed it to one side. He pulled me into an embrace and kissed my forehead. "They'll be perfect," he said. He let go of me, picked up his knife, and got back to his chopping. "If not, we can always put them on the mantelpiece to keep children away from the fire."

I laughed, unable to believe the man's cheek. "Children, you say. Keep making jokes like that, mate, and we won't be having any."

CHAPTER 10

*T*wice I'd tried and failed to curb Mum's zealous approach to my and Leo's wedding. First, at the Cavendish family get-together, and then when she'd turned up with her mood boards. As I drove to my parents' house ready to rein in her enthusiasm yet again, I told myself it was third time lucky. A picture of the newspaper announcement and accompanying photo popped into my head. At least I *hoped* it was third time lucky.

"Well, well, well," I said, smiling as I pulled up outside my childhood home. I usually parked on the drive behind Dad's trusty Volvo, but Dad's car wasn't only missing, it had been replaced. Impressed that Mum's perseverance had finally paid off, I stared at the gleaming metallic-red Mazda MX5. She'd dreamt of owning a sports car for as long as I could remember and while Dad had insisted something so frivolous was just a waste of money, it seemed Mum had, at last, got her wish.

I climbed out of my less than glamorous old runaround, pausing to check out the MX5's luxury, cream leather interior as I made my way towards the house. "Very nice," I said, easily envisaging Mum driving along country road after country road.

Roof back and headscarf on, she'd look every inch the old-school Hollywood star. My smile grew as I realised I'd spent days worrying over nothing. It seemed Mum would be too busy enjoying her new toy to even think about interfering in my wedding plans.

As soon as I let myself into the house, the familiar heady mix of wood polish and carpet freshener assaulted my nostrils. Mum, impeccably dressed as ever, appeared from the lounge to greet me. "Nice car," I said, taking off my jacket and hanging it on the stair banister. "It's very you. I can't believe Dad finally gave in."

Mum looked back at me, confused.

"The Mazda?" I nodded towards the drive.

Mum gave a dismissive wave of her hand, as if a brand-new sports car was nothing. "Oh, that's not mine."

My shoulders slumped. No new car meant no distraction.

Mum, however, smiled. She might not have had new wheels, but she obviously had something thrilling to share. The woman could hardly contain herself.

Guessing it was probably wedding related, I'd hoped to at least sit down with a cup of tea before we got into it. "Where's Dad?" I asked.

Mum's smile slipped. "What do you mean?"

I indicated the front door and driveway beyond. "I didn't see his car."

"That's because…" A facial twitch suddenly appeared under her right eye. "He's out."

Like I hadn't gathered that already.

"Yes. He's off playing golf."

"Really?" According to Mum, Dad had lost touch with everyone he knew and had been under her feet from the day he retired. She was forever insisting he got a hobby so he could make some actual friends and it was nice to know he was finally putting himself out there. "Good for him." Mesmerised by Mum's pulsating tic, I paused in my thoughts. "Mum, are you okay?"

"I'm fine. Why?"

"It's just that…" I pointed to her face.

She put a hand up to try to stop it. "It's because I'm excited." Her smile returned. "Come on through. There's someone I'd like you to meet."

I narrowed my eyes. When I'd arranged to call round, I'd been hoping to have a frank conversation. The last thing I'd anticipated was Mum inviting someone to join us. "Who?"

"Follow me and you'll find out."

Realising I didn't have a choice, I sighed and did as I was told.

"Tess, this is Wendy. Wendy, this is Tess," Mum said, as we entered the living room.

Perched on the edge of a sofa, Wendy rose to greet me. She might have been a few years younger than Mum, but I immediately saw why they were both friends; the two of them were obviously of the same ilk. Wendy's perfectly manicured nails were painted the same shade of red as her lipstick. Wearing cream wide-legged trousers and a simple black shirt, her attire was smart yet casual. And unlike the mess piled on top of my head, she didn't have a hair out of place. "Pleased to meet you," I said, standing there in scruffy jeans and a checked shirt.

"Tea?" Mum asked.

I took in the tray on the coffee table, upon which sat Mum's best crockery and a plate of posh biscuits. "What's the occasion?"

Mum flashed me a look, as if warning me not to embarrass her, and while I rolled my eyes for a second time, wondering what all the fuss was about, she indicated I take a seat on the sofa opposite Wendy's.

"So, you're getting married?" Wendy asked, through brilliant white teeth.

Her question came as no surprise. Having told the whole town about my engagement via her newspaper announcement, I didn't doubt Mum had made it common knowledge within her social circle. "I am."

Wendy tilted her head and smiled. "Have you set a date?"

Mum's eyes widened in anticipation.

"Not yet. We're thinking possibly sometime in September."

"Really?" Mum clapped her hands together in excitement. "An autumn wedding." She sighed, wistful. "How wonderful."

"Next September?" Wendy asked, as she put her cup to her lips.

"No. We're aiming for this year."

In contrast to Mum's delight, Wendy's tea seemed to go down the wrong hole. "But we're already part way through April. You're talking less than six months away, which doesn't leave much time to organise everything."

"I'm sure we'll manage," I replied, wondering what any of it had to do with her.

"You say that now," Mum's friend said, refusing to share my optimism. "But when things start getting double booked…"

I frowned at the woman's patronising tone, but as I opened my mouth to say something Mum clearly sensed my annoyance and jumped in to avoid any discord before I got the chance.

"Wendy's just pointing out how stressful planning a wedding can be." Mum passed me my cup and saucer. "Aren't you, Wendy?"

I reached for a biscuit and much to Mum's clear frustration, defiantly dunked it in my tea.

"I am and understandably so, I might add. What with guest lists, which is always the starting point, by the way. Budgets, and venues–"

"Both for the ceremony and reception," Mum interrupted, sitting next to her friend.

"Photographers and entertainment," Wendy continued.

"Not forgetting a decent florist," Mum said.

My head jerked left and right as I looked from one woman to the other. Sentence after sentence, it was like observing a game of ping-pong.

"And that's on top of finding a decent hairdresser," Wendy said. She paused to look me up and down, her stare going from my head to my toes and back up again. "As well as a good make-up artist."

As if on cue, my soggy biscuit plopped into my tea, while I made a mental note to tell Mum she needed to find a new friend.

"Then there are the bridesmaid dresses to think about," Mum said. "As well as your wedding gown." She gave me a knowing look. "I've got just the one in mind, by the way."

A picture of Louise Patterson popped into my head, causing my whole being to fill with horror. No way was I walking down the aisle looking like an LP copycat. "Same here," I replied, resolute.

Mum froze. "Excuse me?"

"I know which dress I want. It came to me in a dream."

Mum and Wendy looked at me like I was barmy.

"A dream?" Mum said.

I nodded.

"And if you don't find it in real life?" she asked. "What then?"

No way was I losing that challenge. "Believe me, I'll find it."

Mum's expression appeared as unwavering as mine, but ignoring her determination, I took a drink of my tea.

"Then there's the paperwork," Wendy said. "Which has been known to catch people out."

"Paperwork?" I asked, silently questioning why we were even having this conversation.

"The notification of intention to marry," Wendy replied. "No notification, no wedding. You wouldn't believe how many couples forget to get theirs in on time."

I glanced at the woman's left hand. Devoid of any wedding ring, I wondered who made her the nuptial doyen. "You're making everything sound so difficult," I said, hoping to shut Wendy up. "Carry on like this and I might have to call the whole thing off."

Mum let out a hysterical laugh. "Don't be silly." Alarm swept across her face. "We're simply saying there's a lot to consider."

"The perfect wedding does take some organising," her friend said.

I reached for another biscuit, wishing Wendy would leave so I could talk to Mum in private.

"But to have everything just so is more than worth the effort." Wendy smiled. "I'm sure with my expertise, and your mother's support..." She glanced at Mum, her expression ingratiating, before returning her attention to me. "You'll end up with a wonderful day to remember."

Mid-crunch, I wondered what the woman was talking about.

Wendy reached into her handbag and pulled out a notebook and pen. She repositioned herself, her pen poised, ready to begin taking notes. "Shall we get started?"

It was one thing having to deal with Mum's enthusiasm for all things matrimonial, but something else for her to get a friend in on the act too. Questioning what my mother was playing at, I refused to ignore my own ideas for the wedding in favour of giving her the day she wanted.

I looked from one woman to the other and taking in their anticipation, put down my cup and saucer. If there was ever a time to follow Sal's advice on firmness it was then.

"Thank you, Wendy," I said. "I'm sure if Leo and I were going for the whole enchilada, your expertise would be most welcome." I turned to my mother. "And, Mum, while I think it's lovely that you're taking such an interest..." I took in Wendy's pen and pad again. "...along with that of your friend here, Leo and I are more than capable of organising events ourselves. Especially when we're going for a relaxed approach to our day. Something I have previously mentioned."

While Wendy stared at me like I was speaking another language, Mum tried to hide her disappointment.

"That's what I came to talk to you about." I gave Mum a

pointed look. "To make sure one of us isn't getting carried away, like they did over a certain newspaper article."

"I see," Wendy said, although going off her bemusement I wasn't sure she did. "Does this mean you won't be needing my services?"

"Services?" I asked. Yet again, my focus went from one woman to the other.

"Didn't I say?" Mum said, keeping her tone light. "Wendy here is a wedding planner."

I wrinkled my nose and told myself I must have misheard. "Wendy's a what?"

Mum cleared her throat. "A wedding planner."

CHAPTER 11

"I can't believe you embarrassed me like that," Mum said, shutting the front door and heading for the lounge. "What must Wendy think?"

As I followed in Mum's footsteps, I couldn't believe what I was hearing. I was the one who'd been put on the spot, yet Mum was the one playing the victim. "What do you mean, I embarrassed you? Mum, the two of you ambushed me."

"Don't exaggerate."

"How else would you describe it? It's not like anyone told me there was going to be a wedding planner joining us. This little meeting of yours was sprung on me."

"You could have been a bit more polite and said you'd at least think about using her services." Mum began gathering up our used cups and saucers. "Instead of flat out refusing."

Annoyed that Mum couldn't see things from my point of view, I felt my hackles rise. "What would have been the point?" I asked, as I helped place everything back on the tray. "I had no intention of taking her on. And it's not like she needs the business." I pictured Wendy's little red Mazda. "I wish I could afford a car like that."

"Anyone would think I'm wrong for wanting you to have the wedding you deserve." Mum picked up the tray and headed out to the kitchen.

"Mum, it isn't a case of being right or wrong. Or about what anyone deserves." I replied, close behind. "It's about me and Leo getting the kind of wedding we want."

"I was *thinking* of you and Leo. I mean, why not let someone else do all the organising? Let them have all the stress?" She began putting the used crockery into the dishwasher. "You heard what Wendy said. There's a lot to sort out. And now you've decided on a September date... you do realise that's less than six months away?"

Crossing my arms, I leant against the kitchen countertop. "Six months, twelve months, or two years, did it ever cross your mind that we'd like to arrange everything ourselves?"

Mum paused in her actions. "No. It didn't." As she looked at me direct, her expression crumpled. "I'm sorry, Tessa. I don't mean to interfere. It's just this could be the only wedding we have in this family. It's not like Sal's going to be walking down the aisle any time soon."

Mum might have been right about my sister, but that didn't give her the go-ahead to hijack my ceremony. "Which has nothing to do with anything," I said. "And in case you've forgotten you do have a granddaughter. Maybe India will plump for a fancy affair."

Mum looked at me like I'd gone mad. "There's more chance of that girl conquering Everest." Mum sighed. "Don't misunderstand, there's nothing wrong with that. I'd be the first to cheer her on if she did, even if I do think being a lawyer or a doctor is safer and better paid. But every time I think about your wedding, it's like something overtakes me and I can't help but get carried away."

She got back to loading the dishwasher. "I know your sister thinks I'm trying to recreate some celebrity shindig, but she couldn't be more wrong. You getting married isn't about the rich and famous, or me." Her face came over all animated. "Although, let's face it, being mother-of-the-bride is quite an honour."

She shut the dishwasher door and pressed the start button, before giving me her full attention again. "I get excited for you and Leo, as bride and groom. It's like I can see the day happening in my head and I want to turn everything about it into reality. So you can both look back and think *Wow!*"

I recalled Mum's behaviour towards our wedding, thus far. Whatever reel was playing out in her mind, it was evidently nothing like the one in mine. I scoffed to myself, knowing that if I gave in to all Mum's suggestions, *Wow!* would be the exact word to describe our wedding, except not in the way Mum meant. "And we will, Mum. But not because of any castle, or newspaper article, or super-efficient wedding planner like Wendy."

Mum rolled her eyes like a sulky teenager. "Don't I know it!"

A smile crossed my lips as I took in my mother's petulance.

"I miss the old days," she said.

"What are you talking about now?"

"When you and Sal were young. Back then I was involved. Birthdays, Christmas, school plays, no matter the celebration, I got to be a part of them. We all know I'm not the most forthright when it comes to *feelings* and me creating the perfect party or costume was my way of making up for that." Mum let out a sigh. "Like it or not, it still is. What you and your sister call over the top, I call showing I care."

Looking at the woman, I wasn't sure how to respond. Mum had never looked so dejected, let alone opened up like that before.

She sighed. "I knew you wouldn't understand."

"Mum, all we want is to say our vows in front of our closest family and friends. To celebrate with the people we love the most. Isn't that what really matters?"

"I suppose."

"So, does this mean you'll stop with the grand gestures?"

Mum made a noise, accompanied with what may or may not have been a nod.

"I take it that's a *yes*?" I asked.

Again, Mum squeaked and jiggled her head.

"And there'll be no more sudden surprises?"

"No," she said, her voice tight.

"Thank you," I said, glad to hear it.

CHAPTER 12

*T*he visit to my parents' house had been successful on two fronts. Firstly, I could finally stop stressing over Mum, because she'd agreed, albeit grudgingly, to back off from everything matrimonial. And secondly, her and Wendy's verbal ping-pong had galvanised me into action. As soon as I landed home, I'd hit the internet and printed off a wedding checklist for me and Leo to start going through.

I stared at the numerous sheets of paper spread out in front of us. Mum and Wendy hadn't been exaggerating when they'd said there was a lot to think about. Even a less formal affair like the one Leo and I wanted took serious consideration and while Otis lay snoring next to the Aga, we had sat at the kitchen table for hours sharing ideas for the big day itself. Still, the wedding wasn't until September and with copious notes taken and lists drawn in readiness, I could ignore Wendy's warning. It wasn't panic stations yet.

"Shall I make more tea?" I asked. Leo nodded and I got up from my seat. A steady flow of steam rose from the kettle's silver spout and grabbing the quilted potholder I lifted the kettle off the stove. "So, we're happy with numbers?" I asked, as I filled the teapot with boiling water.

We'd decided to invite only our nearest and dearest. On my side, there was Mum and Dad, Sal, Ryan, and India. As well as my two best friends, Abbey and Chloe.

I smiled as I recalled how Abbey and Chloe had jumped up and down screaming when I broke the news of my engagement. I knew my wedding wouldn't be the same without them, so including their partners, and Chloe's daughter, Ruby, that brought my total invitation list to ten.

I watched Leo assess his choice of guests. Like mine, all four of Leo's grandparents were deceased. Leo only had one sibling, his brother, Nial. So when it came to family members, including Nial's wife, Victoria, his parents, Grace, and Bill, that made four. He had a bunch of close friends, and one of them had a son, Tom. Taking into consideration him and the whole group's plus ones, Leo's number of invitations came in at fifteen.

"Twenty-seven total, including us and Otis. I think that's a great number," Leo said.

As I carried the teapot over to the table, I smiled, happily picturing Leo and I saying our *I dos* in front of our most favourite people and dog. Although I couldn't help but think the limited guest list might create an issue. My smile lessened. "Do you think we'll have a problem finding the right venue? I imagine most wedding parties are a lot bigger than ours. And we need somewhere that will facilitate Otis."

Not that that was my only concern. Ever since my dream, I'd set my heart on an outdoor ceremony. In my night-time imagination, everything had seemed perfect, and even days later, I could still see events as they unfolded. Sitting left and right, family and friends rose from lines of white wooden chairs that sat on a perfectly manicured lawn, as the Bridal Chorus kicked in and Dad began walking me down the grassy aisle. Leo, in his waistcoat and trousers, looked as dashing as ever. As did Otis in his little bow tie.

Leo took my hand as I approached, making my whole body tingle as we prepared to exchange vows under a wooden arch that bloomed white thanks to glorious vines of scented Poet's Jasmine. Recalling every detail, I didn't want to settle for anything less. "Then there's the weather. The north of England isn't guaranteed sunshine in July or August, let alone in September."

"What about looking for somewhere with an orangery or a conservatory?" Leo said.

I smiled. "That could work."

"With big double doors that open out onto a beautiful garden."

I let out a dreamy sigh, envisaging a space bathed in light thanks to floor-to-ceiling windows. "Very romantic."

"And if we fill it with flowers, it'll be like bringing the outdoors in."

"Sounds wonderful." I shook myself out of my reverie. "Once the ceremony's over, we could all celebrate with a glass of fizz out on the patio. Then staff can reorganise the room for the reception without any of us lot getting in the way." I indicated our guest list.

"Or at the bar if it's raining."

"I'd like our dining tables to be positioned like this…" I used my fingers to outline a square. "So everyone can see everyone. I don't want any of that top table stuff."

Leo began to write. "Duly noted." He paused to look at me. "Speaking of flowers… That's a job I want to do."

"Really?" Taking in his eagerness, I didn't know why I was so surprised. Leo was an expert when it came to everything flora and fauna, which was why he was always busy on the work front.

"If you're okay with that?"

"Will you have time?" I asked, scrunching my nose up in anticipation. "It's a lot of work."

"I'll make time."

I leaned over and kissed him. "I'd like nothing more."

"Great. I'll put together some designs and you can let me know what you think." He made another note on his pad. "I take it we'll be asking Sal to make the cake?"

"She'll be offended if we don't."

"And what about your mum?"

I cocked my head. "What about her?"

Leo took my hand. "It doesn't seem right to shut her out completely. Don't you think as mother-of-the-bride she should be involved?"

Having only just got the woman in check, the last thing I wanted was her running amok again.

"At least in some small way?" Leo said.

One of the things I loved about Leo was his ability to see the good in everyone. It was also frustrating. Especially when it meant risking our wedding day. After all, Mum had already admitted to getting carried away with things and I wasn't sure if opening that door again was wise. With Leo's determination continuing, I supposed there had to be something Mum could do to help. "How small?" I asked.

Leo's expression softened. "We'll think of something." He let go of my hand, ready to get back to business. "And we're still agreed on the second Saturday in September?"

I nodded. "We are."

Leo reached over. "I can't believe we're actually doing this."

"Neither can I." With butterflies dancing in my tummy at the mere thought of us getting married, goodness knew how I was going to feel when the big day came around. I watched Leo return his attention to his notes. "Leo..." I said, suddenly pensive.

"Yes." He continued to jot things down.

I shifted in my seat. "You're not agreeing to a small wedding for my benefit, are you?"

Leo stopped what he was doing to look at me, but I couldn't bring myself to return his stare. "What makes you ask that?"

I picked up a spoon and stirred my tea. Sal's question about Leo wanting a quiet celebration had kept popping into my head. "Because you're the life and soul," I said. "You enjoy a big party." I pictured how enthralled he was with Mum's big idea mood boards. "I'm the one who prefers everything low-key."

Again, he reached out, this time to turn my face towards him. "Hey, where's all this coming from?"

"I just want to make sure we're not simply doing what *I* want." I took in all the lists we'd made. "I mean it is your wedding too, remember?"

"You're right. I *do* love a big party."

My heart sank.

"But, Tess, this is more than that. We're getting married. The way I see it, we could go all out. Have a grand reception for friends and family, including relatives we haven't seen in years. Then in the evening, invite everyone else we've ever known. But what would be the point? Who would all that effort and expense be for?" He let out a laugh. "Not us."

"You really mean that?"

He rose to his feet and, taking my hands, pulled me onto mine. "I'd be happy heading to the nearest registry office on some random Tuesday afternoon." He wrapped his hands round my waist. "Grabbing some stranger off the street for a witness and walking out as man and wife."

Taking in Leo's earnest expression, I smiled, feeling both relieved and pleased at the same time.

"In fact, how *are* you fixed for this week?"

I laughed at the suggestion. "As romantic as that all sounds, getting married isn't actually that easy."

Leo narrowed his eyes. "What do you mean?"

I wrinkled my nose as I recalled what Wendy had said. "Bureaucracy. We have to submit a notification of intention to marry. Between one and three months before the event."

Appearing almost disappointed, Leo rested his forehead against mine. "Then we'll just have to make do with a posh conservatory in September, won't we?"

CHAPTER 13

MAY

*G*etting our thoughts about the wedding down on paper had done wonders for my productivity. It was as if getting organised had freed up the artistic space in my brain. Day after day, I'd wedged, centred, and thrown, to then turn and trim my creations ready for drying out.

After a busy time in my studio, the last thing I wanted was to spend my Saturday scrubbing the house from top to bottom ready to receive the rest of the Cavendishes. I'd have much preferred to put my feet up and enjoy a few hours with my pencil and drawing pad. I had some designs I wanted to get down, thanks to all the new ideas swirling around my head.

I glanced around the pristine bathroom, knowing that wasn't going to happen, and carrying an empty bottle of bleach and stinking of chlorine, I trudged out onto the landing and made my way downstairs to the kitchen.

Leo was ready and waiting for me with a tin of spray polish and a duster, enough to tell me I wasn't finished on the cleaning front.

"I thought I was done." My whole upper body crumpled. "Can't you just ring and tell them I'm sick?"

He stared at me with a raised eyebrow.

I straightened back up. "But my artistic side is calling."

The man didn't budge.

I fake coughed.

"It'll take you five minutes, Tess." I followed his gaze as he looked over at the kitchen worktop where a beef wellington was set to go in the oven. He turned his attention back to me with a smile. "Unless you want to finish making dinner?"

Not only had cooking never been my forte, I found hosting the Cavendish family get-together stressful enough without having to listen to Mum complain about soggy pastry and raw meat. It wasn't that I didn't enjoy spending time with my family. I simply never had a lot to contribute.

Living out in the sticks and loving the solitude that came with it meant I didn't have much of a social life and being a potter, there weren't many face-to-face dealings with customers to talk about. The Cavendishes might nod in all the right places, but they didn't really want to hear about fettling and luting. I only had to say the term *bisque fire* and everyone's eyes glazed quicker than my pottery.

I swapped the bleach bottle for the proffered cleaning products and turning around, I chunnered to myself, asking why I'd even contemplated marrying such a goody two-shoes as I headed off into the lounge. I stopped in the doorway. *That's why*, I thought. Shaking my head at Leo's silliness, I couldn't help but chuckle thanks to the sight that met me. "Leo," I called out.

Curled up on the rug, Otis lifted his head and looked my way, before settling back down again.

"Could you come here, please?" I put on a pretend stern face and as Leo appeared in the hall, I could see he was doing his best not to giggle too. "What's *that* doing there?" Recalling our conversation about keeping children away from the fire, I pointed to the mantelpiece where the newly framed photo from Mum's newspaper announcement sat loud and proud above the open hearth. "Anything to do with the fact that our eleven-year-old niece is arriving shortly?" I asked. Ignoring the fact that it was springtime, and the fire wasn't lit, I waited for an answer.

Leo tried to swallow his sniggers. "You're going to make me pay for this, aren't you?"

Holding up the polish and duster his way, I fake coughed again.

Leo took them from me. "Go on then. Grab your pencils."

I stretched up and kissed his cheek, before retrieving what I needed off the sideboard ready to lose myself in drawing for a while.

"It's only us," Sal called out. A breeze blew down the hall as my sister, Ryan and India let themselves into the house.

I frowned. "Are we running late?" I asked Leo. "Or are they running early?"

He checked his watch. "A bit of both."

I put my drawing pad and pencils back where they'd been.

"Dinner won't be long, will it?" Ryan asked, as they all took their jackets off and hung them on the coat stand. "I've been saving myself all day. I'm starving."

As they filed down the hall to the kitchen, my disappointment was fast replaced. My jaw dropped at the sight of my niece as they passed. Seeing that the white scientist coat was no more, I looked to Leo, who shrugged, as much in the dark as me.

"Don't ask," Sal said, as I opened my mouth to speak.

I couldn't take my eyes off India as Leo and I followed in their footsteps. She wore black shoes, thick black tights, and a long black velvet dress. Her ensemble was topped off with a sheer black veil that covered her whole head and shoulders. She looked like she'd just stepped out of a Stephen King horror novel. Even the way she walked had an unsettling sombreness to it.

"Very gothic," Leo said.

"Very something," I replied, keeping my voice low.

"She's trying out a new job," Ryan said, as he, Sal and India settled themselves at the table. "After the garden experiment we thought it best."

Sal smiled through gritted teeth.

"What kind of job?" I asked, as Leo got back to the cooking. Her outfit wasn't like any uniform I'd seen before.

"Isn't it obvious?" India said.

Thanks to her shroud I might not have seen the girl's scorn, but I heard it.

"I'm a professional mourner."

"Of course you are," I replied, unaware that that was even a thing. "Silly me."

"A role that originates from a variety of cultures: Egyptian, Chinese, Mediterranean and Near Eastern..." India said.

"And very proficient you look too," Leo said.

I stared at the man, wondering what was wrong with him. In his shoes, I'd be calling off the wedding and running back to Cumbria. We Cavendishes might be a mad bunch, but as career choices went, no one could deny that lamenting for money was frankly bizarre.

"I knew you'd get it." India smiled at Leo. "Would you like to hear my wail?"

"No!" Sal and Ryan called out. They had clearly heard enough of their daughter's bogus grieving.

I headed to the fridge for a bottle of wine. "Drink, anyone?"

My sister's hand shot up. "Yes, please."

"Not for me," Ryan said. He frowned at Sal. "It's my turn to drive."

"So, how are the wedding plans coming along?" Sal asked.

"Very well," Leo said. "We've pinned down a date."

"Second Saturday in September," I said, as I grappled with the corkscrew.

"Brilliant," Ryan said. "Any ideas on a venue."

"We've made a shortlist," I replied. "Although we need to

properly check them out. Make sure they're as good as they appear on their websites."

My sister gave us both a big smile. "You *are* getting organised."

"Actually," I said. "We were hoping you'd make our wedding cake?"

Sal squealed. "You bet I will. Have you got any designs in mind? It doesn't matter if you don't, I'm sure between us we'll come up with something fabulous."

I knew Sal would be happy we'd asked but considering she didn't believe in marriage her excitement came as a surprise. "Also…" I screwed up my face in anticipation. With Abbey and Chloe having to step aside, I didn't think I could face another disappointment. "If you'd be our matron of honour?"

Sal looked back at me, as if not sure what to say.

"It's okay if you don't want to," Leo said. "We respect your views. We just thought we'd give you the choice."

"Duh, of course I'll do it."

"You will?" I asked.

Sal grinned. "Marriage might not be for me, but that doesn't mean I can't be a part of yours."

"You don't need time to think about it?"

My sister scoffed. "What is there to think about?"

Astounded by how easy that was, I shook my head, before turning to my niece. "And, India," I said, with a smile, "we thought you might like to be bridesmaid?"

India's hand flew up and she flipped her veil back.

My smile vanished.

She stared at me, her expression blank. "Why?"

As I stared at her, it was a question I found myself asking. India's face was covered in white powder, and she wore smudged mascara and smeared red lipstick. Together with the black, her whole ensemble looked horrific and wondering what was wrong with the girl, I wished I hadn't opened my mouth. Lost for words, I looked to Leo for assistance.

"Well, you seem to have nailed the funeral market," he said, matter of fact. "Why not branch out into weddings?"

"So, you're saying I'll get paid?"

Sal glanced my way, her face full of sympathy. "I'm sorry," she mouthed.

"I'm sure we can work something out," Leo said.

"Okay," India replied. "I'll let you know my terms and conditions nearer the time."

Great! I thought, as I listened to them. On the one hand, I had a niece demanding money before she'd even consider taking part in my wedding. While on the other, I had a mother who couldn't help herself and was aiming for wedding of the year.

"Yoo hoo!" Mum called out.

As I continued to question what was wrong with my family, I braced myself in readiness of yet more madness.

CHAPTER 14

"It's only us." Sounding my parents' arrival with her usual greeting, Mum scanned the room as the two of them entered. Her expression froze as her eyes settled on India. She put a hand up to stop anyone who might speak. "Don't tell me. I don't want to know." She turned to Dad who, in contrast, stood there chuckling at the sight of his granddaughter.

The rest of us tried not to laugh as Mum took a moment to compose herself. "So, what is it this time?" she finally asked.

"Professional mourner," those of us in the know all said.

Mum let out a long despondent sigh. "What is it with this family, Edward? We're never going to get a lawyer or a doctor, are we?" She turned to look at India again. "At this point I'd settle for an accountant."

I clocked Dad and his granddaughter share a knowing look, forcing me to wonder if it was Dad who'd put the idea into the girl's head. I wouldn't have put it past him. He'd been equally as mischievous when Sal and I were young. From giving us an extra biscuit when Mum wasn't looking, to not just letting us choose our own bedroom designs but helping with the painting too, Dad wasn't only fun, he was naughty. He had to have known Mum would go nuts over the latter and while my sister and I could decry *but Dad said*, he certainly had no excuse.

I pictured Mum the day she landed home all those years ago. After spending a relaxing week away with friends, she was delighted to hear that Dad had used the time to get on with some DIY and was keen to see his handiwork. Upon entering Sal's room, Mum was overjoyed. White walls, white bedding, white wardrobes and drawers, my sister had taken minimalist to the extreme. Unlike me, who'd gone for the opposite approach.

Proud of my more personal design scheme, I couldn't wait for Mum to see it. However, her happy squeals ended when she saw my choice of colour palette. I remembered my confusion when she grabbed the door handle to steady herself once she stepped into my kaleidoscope of reds, blues, purples and yellows...

Mum's less than enamoured response was understandable. My room was awful. But her instructing Dad to replace it with magnolia was like whitewashing over my personality, even if, as Mum rightly claimed, it did provide for a better sleep.

Shaking away the memory, I grabbed some glasses and poured the wine, while Leo got Ryan, India, and Dad an orange juice.

"Cheers," Leo said, as he and I sat down with everyone.

"Cheers!" We all raised our glasses in response.

The room fell quiet, and an uneasiness descended. It was the first time I'd come face to face with Mum since she and Wendy the wedding planner had bushwhacked me. I could still feel the awkwardness as Wendy had lowered herself into her MX5, while Mum and I stood at the front door waving her off.

All three of us wore fixed smiles, pretending the morning hadn't really been a waste of everyone's time. After that, I might have asked Mum to back off when it came to all things matrimonial, but I hadn't banned her from talking about them. I'd still expected the wedding to be her first topic of conversation.

I certainly hadn't anticipated everyone's radio silence on the matter. Even Sal and Ryan had stopped chatting. I assumed for my benefit. It was as if Mum's prior behaviour, and, ergo, my impending nuptials, had suddenly become an elephant in the room and as we all sat exchanging uncomfortable smiles, I wondered if that was how it was going to be from then on. Everyone too scared to make small talk should the subject of my wedding come up and send Mum into exuberant overdrive.

I glanced at Leo, who reached for my hand under the table. He gave it a squeeze and discreetly nodded Mum's way as if I should say something to her.

Realising I didn't exactly have a choice, I gathered myself ready to break the ridiculous silence. "About the wedding, Mum," I began.

Ryan leaned towards Sal. "Here we go."

Evidently not wanting to miss a word of my and Mum's exchange, my sister shushed him.

Mum's eyes lit up and she opened her mouth to say something.

"Patricia?" Dad said, before she could get her words out.

Mum turned to look at him, clearly irritated by the interruption.

"Remember what we talked about?" he said, keeping his voice calm.

"But she brought up the subject."

Dad gave Mum a look and heeding his warning, her shoulders slumped.

"It's all right, Dad," I said.

I felt Leo squeeze my hand for a second time and knowing I could be about to lose any control I had over Mum, I steeled myself in readiness. "We just wanted to ask…"

"Yes?" Mum said, her eagerness there for all to see.

"Well, we wondered if you'd like to take charge of the

invitations?" I said. "You know, sending them out and keeping tabs on the RSVPs."

Mum's whole demeanour changed. A smile slowly spread across her face as she turned to Dad. "See. Didn't I tell you they'd come round?"

"Come round to what?" I asked.

"Nothing," Mum said.

"Because if you're planning on getting ahead of yourself again."

"I'm not."

"You've set a date then?" Dad asked, no doubt before Mum could drop herself in it.

"Second Saturday in September," Leo replied.

Dad smiled. "An autumn wedding? How lovely."

"Am I responsible for choosing the design too?" Mum asked, not yet ready to let the conversation properly move on. "After all, traditionally, wedding invites do come from the bride's parents and not the happy couple."

Ryan clamped down on his jaw, as if trying not to laugh.

"I don't see why not," Leo said.

"What do you think, Tess?" Leo looked at me with an encouraging smile. "Are you all right with that?"

My sister's eyes drilled into me. She discreetly shook her head, willing me to say no.

I understood why. We both knew what Mum could be like and Sal had always met Mum's overbearing personality head on. She challenged it by being just as forceful. Unlike me, who, more often than not, chose my battles. The morning I met Wendy, the wedding planner, popped into my head again and I recalled Mum telling me how being involved in our wedding was her way of showing Leo and I how much she cared. Under that circumstance, denying her request felt cruel.

"I don't see…" Suddenly remembering Mum's mood boards, images of gold leaf lettering, hand-drawn laurel wreaths, and wax-sealed envelopes flooded my brain. My voice cracked, forcing me to clear my throat. "…why not."

Sal slumped in her seat, her disappointment in my response evident.

Mum clapped her hands. "Wonderful. I can't wait to get started."

"Just keep us up to date with everything," I said, making it clear that we'd be monitoring her.

"Oh, I will. And thank you," Mum replied. "You don't know how much this means to me."

"I think we do," Ryan said with a snigger.

"And don't worry," Mum carried on. "Your invites are safe with me."

No doubt glad it would keep Mum from grumbling and therefore off his back, Dad gave me an appreciative wink, while India straightened herself up in her seat. "Does this mean I can choose my own bridesmaid dress?" she asked.

Her question caught me off guard and as I took in India's attire, I swallowed hard. Unsure how to respond, I might not have wanted all the pomp and ceremony when it came to my wedding, but that didn't mean I was happy with Wednesday Addams following me down the aisle.

"I mean, if Grandma gets to choose what invites she wants it's only fair I get a say in what I wear."

"I can't see a problem with that," Leo said.

My husband-to-be clearly hadn't only gone mad, he'd gone blind.

"I think a meeting's in order," Mum said.

"For what?" I replied.

"Well, if we're talking dresses, we still have yours to think about."

I cringed at the word *we.*

"And I did tell you I have just the gown in mind," Mum said. "Remember?"

"You let her back in," Sal said under her breath.

"And like I explained to you, Mum, *I* already have another design in mind."

Ignoring my words, Mum reached into her handbag and pulled out her diary.

"So there really is no point..." As Mum flicked through the pages, it was clear I was talking to myself.

"How're you fixed for next Friday?"

Throwing my arms in the air, I looked to Leo for assistance, but none was forthcoming and I wondered why I'd listened to him in the first place regarding Mum's involvement. As usual, he seemed happy to go with the flow. I turned my attention to the others. But with Dad shrugging sympathetically, Ryan struggling to contain his amusement, and Sal giving me one of her 'I told you so' looks, it seemed I was on my own.

"Well?" my mother said, eager for an answer.

I let out a long, drawn-out sigh. When it came to reining in my mother's matrimonial fervour, it seemed I was, indeed, back to square one.

CHAPTER 15

Friday arrived far too quickly. All blue skies and sunshine, it was a gorgeous, bright spring day and would have been perfect for spending it at home, in my workshop, with the door wide open so I could breathe in the scent of the garden while I worked. The whole area around the cottage was starting to come to life.

Thanks to Leo's hard labour, there was an array of flora and fauna to enjoy. Butterflies danced and bees buzzed from one colourful profusion to another. Roses, foxgloves, daisies, and violets mingled with berry and fruit trees, sage, lavender, and thyme; the latter planted for their use as much as their aesthetic value.

Then again, I also had a wedding to arrange and with everything yet to properly organise, I supposed it was time to start getting on with it and having collected Sal, as I concentrated on the road, she sat, arms folded and head back, in the passenger seat. She let out a long yawn and glancing her way, her sunglasses didn't fool me; I knew my sister's eyes were closed. "Late night?" I asked.

"You could say that. I had a giant birthday cake to finish. The client's collecting it this morning. Days earlier than planned."

"Don't you need to be there?"

"Ryan can handle it." She turned her head to look at me. "This is way more important."

I scoffed. "Is that you speaking? Or Mum?"

"Mum. She insisted I come." Sal smiled. "Apparently, it's my duty as matron of honour."

"Why do you think she keeps doing these things? It's not like I haven't asked her to stop. She's like a bridezilla without being the bride."

"Maybe she meant what she said and just wants the best for you?"

As much as I wanted to believe that, I still wasn't sure. "You think?"

"As well as to outdo the local celebrity."

I flicked on the car indicator and, slowing to make my turn, brought the car to a standstill on Mum and Dad's driveway. Sitting in silence, Sal and I stared up at the house. The huge semi-detached looked the same as it had always done – grand, imposing, and covered in far too much ivy.

Blocking out the sun, the property cast an enormous shadow straight over us. I dreaded what I was about to be met with. Mum might nod in all the right places when it came to accepting the fact that Leo and I were having a small wedding, but her actions continued to show she had the opposite in mind.

"I still don't understand why she wants us both here," my sister said. "It's not like I'm an expert on wedding dresses."

"Well I, for one, am glad you've come," I said. "I need the reinforcements. No matter what I say, nothing seems to stop the woman. She says she gets it, then steamrolls right over me."

I recalled my last visit to Mum's house, when she and Wendy, the wedding planner, had been lying in wait. I wouldn't have put it past Mum to pull a similar stunt and I began to feel a mix of nerves and irritation as I pictured her and some wedding boutique owner standing proud in the living room next to a rail of white and ivory gowns. Instead of Mum's best crockery, I saw an ice bucket, home to a bottle of the best champagne, and a tray of canapés rather than a plate of posh biscuits.

"It's your duty to protect me," I said, like Mum had done, pulling the matron of honour card. I looked around, glad to find my immediate surroundings devoid of little white vans with names like *Wedding Belles* and *Forevermore Frocks* plastered across their sides. I turned off the engine and pulled the key out of the ignition.

"I don't get the need for a discussion to start with," Sal said. "It would've been much more fun to meet at the bridal shop. At least there you get to try dresses on." My sister turned to look at me, a mischievous smile appearing on her lips. "Unless she's done another mood board? Because that I'd love to see." Sal came over all animated. "I can already picture it." She held up her hands. "A massive collage of lace and silk and embroidery."

"Then she'll have wasted her time. Lace and embroidery are far too fussy for me. Besides, I already know the kind of dress I want. And it's not the Louise Patterson knock-off Mum has in mind."

Sal looked at me aghast. "Since when? I thought that was just an excuse to get Mum off your back."

"Since it came to me in a dream."

"And you think Mum's batty."

Ignoring my sister's quip, I reached down into the passenger footwell for my bag and pulled out my sketchpad. Excitement enveloped me as I turned the pages until I found what I was looking for. Eager to share my imagined design, I handed the whole thing over.

My sister studied the drawing.

"Well?" I wrinkled my nose and held my breath as I awaited her verdict.

Sal's eyes widened and a smile spread across her face as she took in the tea-length dress with its flared skirt, three quarter sleeves, and deep V neckline. "This is gorgeous."

Relieved she loved it as much as I did, I, at last, exhaled.

Sal leaned over and threw her arms around me. "You're going to look stunning. Even Mum won't be able to deny how perfect this is."

I admired my sister's optimism, again wanting to believe her.

She released her grip. "I still can't believe my little sister's getting married."

"Me neither. Sometimes I have to pinch myself to make sure I'm awake."

Sal turned her attention back to the sketch. "So, where do we find this dress of yours?"

Considering Sal's views when it came to marriage, her enthusiasm continued to shock me. I shrugged. "I've looked online, but nowhere seems to stock anything like it."

"Hardly surprising considering it's come out of your head."

"Please don't tell Mum I'm struggling. The last thing I want is her having an *in* to dictate what gown I wear. Which is probably why she wants you here too. To get you on side when it comes to her vision of the perfect wedding dress."

"Like that's going to happen. I've never known me and Mum agree on anything. Besides..." Sal took another look at my design. "This is definitely the one for you."

"Thanks, Sal. Your support means a lot."

"What are big sisters for?" She handed me my pad back and indicated the car door. "Come on. We've sat here long enough. Anyway, my money's still on Mum showing us another mood board."

$\mathcal{A}$s we alighted the vehicle and headed for the house, Sal and I chuckled at the prospect of yet more collages from Mum. Before we'd even reached the front door it flew open to reveal the woman eagerly waiting to greet us. She wore a smile as bright as that morning's sunshine and an enthusiastic expression I recognised all too well. I slowed in my step, reluctant to enter.

"Good morning, you two," Mum said. "I hope you're in the mood for a bit of fun this fine day." Gesturing us inside, she guided Sal and a suspicious me into the lounge.

"What's all this?" My sister nodded to the coffee table where an ice bucket containing a bottle of champagne sat in readiness. Heading over, she checked the bottle's label. "Very nice."

I scanned the rest of the room, relieved to find my prior misgivings hadn't been fully realised. Despite the presence of alcohol, there was no gown rail in sight.

"We can't talk wedding dresses without a bit of fizz," Mum said. Making straight for the ice bucket, she poured us each a glass. She held hers up, encouraging Sal and me to follow suit.

"Cheers!" we all said.

Being the one with the car keys and as a result, the designated driver, I put my glass down. "No Dad today?"

"No." Mum's smile appeared to slip. "He's out and about."

"Developing his swing?"

"Well, this is a *ladies-only* occasion," she said.

Mum's eye started twitching, making me wonder if I should be worried and concerned Mum's excitement over the wedding was starting to affect her neurons, I looked to Sal to see if she'd clocked it too. However, busy settling herself on the sofa, my sister didn't appear to have, and putting my fears to one side, I retrieved my sketchpad from my bag and sat down.

"So where are we with the organising?" Mum said, also taking a seat.

I flinched at her use of the word *we*, something she'd taken to saying of late. "All on track. We've booked to go and look at what sounds like the perfect venue next week."

"How exciting." Mum's face lit up, as she grabbed her diary and a pen from behind the cushion next to her.

I rolled my eyes. The diary and pen had evidently been strategically placed.

"When next week?" Mum said. "And where?" She licked her finger, before using it to flick through to the required page. After writing the words *WEDDING VENUE* and underlining them, she sat poised, ready to record the details.

"Mum, why do you need to know this?" I asked.

"So I can come with you, of course. Unless you don't want me there?"

"Well..."

She let out a pitiful sigh. "I mean, as you keep telling me, I'm *only* the bride's mother."

Throughout all our discussions, those words had never left my lips. However, as I opened my mouth to tell her that, the woman looked so pathetic I couldn't bring myself to speak. Of course, I knew her demeanour was a ploy, but that didn't stop me from feeling guilty. Mum took such pleasure from my wedding plans and having not seen her that excited in years, raining on her parade yet again didn't sit right. A little voice reminded me that I needed to push back. That my upcoming marriage wasn't about her.

"I thought we were here to talk wedding dresses," Sal said, coming to my rescue. She picked up the champagne bottle and poured herself another glass. "Because Tess has…"

"You're right," Mum said. Placing the pen and pad to one side, she straightened up in her seat and took a deep breath. "Tessa, darling, I have a surprise for you."

Terror enveloped me. "What kind of surprise?"

She rose to her feet. "Could you come with me, please."

"Where are we going?" Panic-stricken, I turned to Sal. My eyes pleaded for more assistance, but none was forthcoming. Wearing a hint of a smile, my sister simply shrugged, as if there was nothing more she could do. "Some matron of honour you are," I said, keeping my voice down.

Mum took my arm and led me out into the hall. "You first," she said, indicating we head upstairs.

With an idea as to the horror about to befall me, my feet felt like lead.

"Chop, chop!" Mum said, nudging me forward.

I put my hand on the banister and began making my ascent. Step by step, it felt like I was marching to a death knell.

We reached the landing and as Mum indicated her and Dad's bedroom, I stalled, not wanting to enter.

Mum grabbed the door handle and swung it open for me, making it clear I didn't have a choice. "After you," she said.

Steeling myself, I crossed the threshold, only to realise that my fears did not do the situation justice. Speechless, I stared at the massive explosion of fabric hanging against the wardrobe door and while Mum squealed in delight, I'd never seen anything so appalling. "Incredible," I said, at last.

Mum clapped her hands in excitement. "I knew you'd love it."

I let out a whimper.

Pulling me further into the room, Mum's happiness continued. "I did that too when I first saw it. Perfection can have that effect." She placed an arm around my shoulders, preventing me from doing a running jump at the window. "And when I first put it on…" Mum came over all wistful. "I felt just like a princess."

"This is *your* wedding dress?" I asked. Talk about putting me in a predicament.

Mum nodded, while I wanted to cry. "And now it's yours," she said, whether I wanted it or not. "I always hoped to pass it on to you or your sister. You know, like a family heirloom that goes from generation to generation."

She reached out to touch the fabric, then turned to me, her expression earnest. "To have you walk down the aisle in my own gown would be an absolute honour."

CHAPTER 17

*M*um had left me to change in private and as I stood there alone in the silence, I stared at my reflection, lost for words. Mum's freestanding mirror demonstrated all too well the gown's full effect and it wasn't pretty. Despair overwhelmed me as I took in the vision of awfulness. I looked like a head and two arms poking out of a humongous pearl and sequinned meringue. The dress's bodice was frilled with lace, while yet more flounces adorned the neckline and sleeves. As I frowned at the embroidered heart motif decorating the chest, it seemed everything about the dress was wrong.

My gaze settled on the reflection of the veil lying on the bed behind me. Goodness knew what I'd turn into when that went on.

My eyes widened as one of the world's most iconic moments suddenly flashed through my mind. "Please, God, no." Horrified, I didn't know whether to laugh or cry. "Mum, you can't do this to me."

A tap on the bedroom door diverted my anguish and I spun round, desperate. Without the right words to let her down gently, the last thing I wanted was Mum telling me how beautiful the ensemble was.

"Are you decent?" Sal asked.

Relief swept over me. Never had I been so glad to hear my sister's voice. If anyone could get me out of the mess I was in, it was Sal.

"It's just that Mum's wondering what's taking you so long."

"If you mean, am I dressed? Then the answer's yes." I steeled myself ready for Sal's reaction as the door opened, and she stepped into the room.

"And abracadabra I'm back in the eighties."

I wished my sister was referring to Mum's pale green carpet, peach floral bedding, and not very convincing wood-effect laminate wardrobes, but she'd yet to take her eyes off me.

"You look so… so…" She sat on the bed.

"Regal?"

Sal put the back of her hand up to her mouth, her eyes wide in stunned recognition. Her hand fell to her chest. "Oh. My. God. Yes, that's it!"

My attention was drawn to the dress's skirt when something scratchy irritated my thigh. Forced to fight with the excess fabric in order seek out the problem, I hoisted it all up and wrangled it over my arm.

"What are you doing?" my sister asked.

"Something's bothering me." I frowned as I finally located the issue. "Looks like a dry-cleaning ticket." I assessed the faded tag, before letting the skirt fall again, ready to get back to the matter at hand. "What am I going to do, Sal?" I asked. "I can't walk down the aisle in the same gown as…"

Sal put a hand up to silence me. "Please don't say it."

"…Princess Diana."

My sister struggled to contain herself.

"Even Louise Patterson's dress was better than this."

A snigger escaped Sal's lips.

"One look at me and Leo's going to run a mile."

Sal's sniggering got worse. "Honestly, you really do need to stop."

"I'm telling you, he'll ditch me before I reach the altar."

Try as she might to stop herself, my sister burst into laughter.

"Sal, this isn't funny."

"I'm sorry, Tess, but yes it is." Her eyes spied the metres of veil I'd yet to try on.

"Oh no," I said, knowing exactly what Sal was about to suggest. "No chance."

"Go on. Just for me." She rose from her seat. "In fact, let me help." She fiddled with the veil's comb slide and fabric to secure it in place. Continuing to snicker, Sal stepped back to get a proper look, before producing her mobile from her back pocket.

"What are you doing?" I asked, as she swiped the screen.

"Taking a picture."

"You can't!"

Ignoring my protests, she held up her phone. "Ryan's going to love this. Come on, Tess. Smile."

Standing there, I wished I had something to smile about.

Tapping the button, Sal checked the result and delighted with the shot, handed me the mobile. "What do you think?" she asked, amused. "Better than your simple tea-style dress?"

Humiliation swept over me. The phone image was worse than the one in the mirror. I visualised my wedding day, but, unlike in my dream, when guests had looked upon me as a vision of beauty, everyone stared at me open mouthed and in shock. Except Mum, who dabbed glistening tears from her joyful eyes. "Why is she doing this to me?" I asked.

Sal started tittering again.

"This is a nightmare," I said.

Sal's titters turned into full-blown laughter. "I'm sorry. It's just…" She took another look at me, struggling to speak. "I've never seen anything like it."

I cocked my head and raised an eyebrow, reminding her that, in fact, she had, even if it was via a TV screen back in 1981.

Sal bent double in response and full-on guffawing, clutched her stomach. "I mean it, Tess. I can't take any more."

"You can't? How do you think I feel right now? As much as I don't want to hurt Mum's feelings, you have to help me, Sal. I need an excuse not to wear it."

"Such as?"

"I don't know. We could tell her that I'm allergic to taffeta?"

Sal laughed some more.

"Or that ivory doesn't favour my skin?"

"Like she's going to accept that."

"Mum'll never forgive us if she knows we hate it."

"What's this *we* business?"

"So you'd actually wear this, would you?"

Sal sniggered again. "I don't have to. I don't believe in marriage."

"Yoo hoo!"

We froze at the sound of my mother's voice.

"Jesus, Sal, what am I gonna do?" Keeping my voice low, I indicated the door. "Mum might've been happy to play royalty for a day, but I'm not."

Sal started to chuckle again. "I think I'm going to wee myself." Sensing our mother's approach, my sister suddenly sat up straight. She swallowed, and like a naughty child, did her utmost to compose herself as Mum flounced into the room.

"Oh, Tessa. You look…" She put a hand up to her chest. "…like a princess."

A squeal escaped my sister's mouth, and as I willed her not to break down in another fit of laughter, it was clear Sal was on the verge of losing control. Thankfully her mobile rang before she properly let slip her thoughts on the dress. "It's the school," Sal said, her voice cracking. She pointed to the door and landing beyond. "I should probably take this."

"Please, go ahead," I replied, relieved to have her out of the way.

I turned to Mum, and realising I had no choice but to be straight with her, I indicated we sit. As I prepared to speak, Mum looked at me with a mix of pride and delight. I felt like the shittest daughter on the planet thanks to the conversation I was about to have, but heirloom or not, no way could I get married in a Princess Diana dress. "About this..." I looked down at the mounds of fabric I was cocooned in. "...creation."

"Beautiful, isn't it?"

"I really appreciate you wanting me to–"

Sal burst back into the room, before I could finish. "Sorry to interrupt," she said, her face serious. "But there's been an incident. I have to go and collect India."

"Is she all right?" Mum asked. "What kind of incident?"

"The erm... class gerbil's died."

"I see," Mum said. Although her confused expression highlighted the fact that she didn't. Horror swept across her face. "India didn't kill it, did she?"

"No." Sal gasped. "How could you ask that?"

In my mind it was a fair question.

Sal sighed. "If you must know, she saw the death as an opportunity to practice her mourning skills."

"You're joking," I said.

"Worse than that, it would seem she has a talent for it. According to the head, my daughter's wailing was so realistic the whole class is in tears."

Picturing the scene, it was my turn to hide my amusement.

"Twenty-odd children, all bawling and howling." Sal shook her head. "I swear she gets it all from her father."

Sat there in a replica Princess Diana dress, next to a mother who couldn't see what was wrong with that, I wasn't so sure.

"Tess, are you all right giving me a lift?"

Realising India had bought me some time to organise my

thoughts, which meant my conversation with Mum could wait, I nodded and rose to my feet. "Just let me get out of this." I looked down at Mum's wedding-dress-come-heirloom, determined never to set eyes on it again.

However, as Mum stood up too it was clear she had other ideas. She headed for her wardrobe and pulled out a humongous garment bag. "Hurry up." She indicated the gown. "I need to pack that up so you can take it with you."

CHAPTER 18

*L*eo reached over and squeezed my hand as we drove down the seemingly endless drive. "I'm looking forward to this."

"Me too," I replied, slouched in my seat.

Leo raised an eyebrow, as he glanced my way. "You don't look like you are. Otis appears more excited."

I twisted round to see Otis with his head poking out of the rear door window. His jowls flapped about as the wind hit his face and I managed a smile at the sight, before returning my attention to the road in front. Checking out our potential wedding venue should have been a welcome distraction. However, try as I might, I couldn't get the dilemma of Mum's Princess Diana heirloom out of my head. "I'm just thinking."

"About?"

I cocked my head, unable to believe he had to ask.

"Ah. The dress."

I scowled. "It's not a dress, Leo. It's a cross between a giant meringue and an embroidered yurt."

Leo tried not to laugh. "It can't be that bad."

"You wanna bet?"

"It's a great gesture though, don't you think? Passing something down the generations like that."

I sighed, wondering why Leo had to be so nice about everything. "I get the sentiment. Why do you think I feel in such a dilemma? But it's all right for you. You don't have to wear it."

"Neither do you," Leo said.

He might have been right, but that didn't make turning my mother's offer down any easier. "You didn't see Mum's face when I put it on. You'd have thought we were looking at two different gowns." I stared out of the window. Taking in the age-old trees surrounding us, our destination seemed to be in the middle of a forest. "I can't believe the way she's trying to hijack everything. If you ask me, the woman's not normal." I fell silent for a moment. "I bet your mum wouldn't behave like mine."

"Patricia's just being Patricia."

I stared at the man, unimpressed. Having guilted me into letting Mum get involved in the first place, it was his fault I was in such a mess. "I can't help thinking there's more to it."

"Like what?"

I took a deep breath and exhaled. "Oh, don't mind me. I'm probably overreacting. Mum's always been a bit too zealous when it comes to family celebrations." I thought back to mine and Sal's childhood. "Take birthday parties. I bet when you were young, you had cheese and ham, or egg and cress sandwiches for lunch, followed by jelly and ice cream. Stuff that children actually like."

"I did."

"Do you know what Mum put on for us and our friends? Canapés. Bitesize sweetcorn fritters with avocado salsa."

Leo shook his head. "Please tell me you're exaggerating."

For the first time since leaving the house, my face broke into a smile. "I wish I was."

"Very sophisticated."

"Which is exactly what Mum said at the time." I scoffed.

"Believe me, the concept behind goat cheese and walnut tartlets is lost on a bunch of eight-year-olds. The stick Sal and I got thanks to Mum's party food. Now she wants me to be a laughing stock on what should be the best day of my life."

My mobile bleeped and I reached down into the footwell to retrieve it from my bag. Unable to help but smirk, I shook my head at the incoming photo that had landed. "Even Abbey and Chloe find the whole thing hilarious. Do you know how many wedding gown memes they've sent through? My phone's full of them."

Leo chuckled, while I stuffed my mobile away again. "Why don't we forget about Patricia and her dress for now?"

That was easy for him to say.

"And focus on something positive. Like why we're here."

Seeing Leo's hopeful expression, I suddenly felt guilty. There we were, about to tour our number-one wedding venue, and I'd spent the whole journey there doing nothing but grumble. I straightened in my seat, determined to perk up. "You're right. Today is about having a great day out while doing something constructive."

Leo smiled. "That's my girl," he said, as we carried on down the drive.

"Oh my word," I said. As Gregbrook Manor, at last, rose in the distance, all my worries immediately vanished. "Look at the place... It's massive."

Leo stared ahead, equally impressed. "Wow! I did not expect that."

As we approached, the building was both dramatic and enchanting. A Victorian gothic mansion, with huge turrets and limestone mullion bay windows, it exuded grandeur and romance. Before Leo had even pulled up, my seat belt was off. I couldn't wait to get inside. And neither could Otis, who bounced around and whined, desperate to go exploring.

We jumped out of the car and clipping Otis onto his lead,

headed for the entrance. Coming to a standstill in the giant stone porch, we were awed by the sight that met us. The area was double ceiling height, from which hung a modern, black and glass, six-bulb light fitting. The floor was tiled in a simple geometric pattern, which contrasted perfectly with the pale limestone walls. Well-stocked, fresh flower displays brimmed with colour and countless pairs of yellow wellington boots lined the shelves of an ancient storage unit; no doubt, for guests to avail themselves of. Having read on their website that there were thirty acres of grounds, I thought the wellies were a great touch. The owners were obviously keen for visitors to go exploring.

Leaving the porch behind, we led Otis into the main foyer. With an enormous reception desk lining the far end, grey Chesterfield sofas and tan leather armchairs sat to the left. While to the right, there was an imposing wooden turn staircase that wound its way upwards.

As I moved to take a closer look, my regard lifted skyward. The stairway appeared never ending as it snaked from floor to floor to floor. I stroked the well-worn banister. "I'd put money on this being original."

Continuing to soak up my surroundings, for all its olde worlde charm, the space also had a contemporary, almost jovial, feel. Thanks to pieces like the bronze top-hatted deer head that hung high on the wall.

"So far, so good," Leo said.

"Better than that," I said. "It's perfect." I took Leo's hand and pulled him and the dog towards the bank of receptionists. "Next stop, the orangery."

CHAPTER 19

*L*eo smiled my way as he guided Otis onto the back seat, but no matter how much he tried to hide the fact, I knew he was as disappointed as I was. Letting ourselves into the front of the vehicle, Leo and I sat in silence for a moment. We sighed as we stared straight ahead.

"There'll be other places," Leo finally said.

"There will."

"Places just as good as this, if not better."

"I agree."

"We've simply got to find them."

"We do."

Wallowing in our disenchantment, we both let out a longer, more mournful, sigh.

"Gregbrook Manor *is* to die for though," I said.

"It is."

"And that orangery. It's so beautiful." Like the ones in my imagination, it cascaded with natural light. "All those glass panels..."

"What about its glass-domed roof?" Leo said. "I've never seen anything like it."

"Me neither."

"And I really like the walled courtyard."

"Me too." As with the manor's interior, its exterior was a mix of old and new and I happily pictured its magnificent magnolia trees, still able to hear the babbling water that flowed from the beautiful French fountain. I could smell the soft fragrance of the rambling roses that snaked around the wrought-iron pergola. In my mind's eye, I had no problem envisaging our wedding party, champagne glasses in hand, flitting seamlessly from one space to the other. Which, sadly, was never going to happen.

"Why did everything have to be so big?" Leo asked.

It was a question I kept asking myself. Set up to host over a hundred guests, the orangery didn't exactly scream intimate. And although perfect in every other sense, it was way too large for our party of twenty-seven.

"Time to focus on the next venue on our list?" Leo asked.

I nodded. "I'm afraid so."

CHAPTER 20

The weekend trip out to Gregbrook Manor had left Leo and me feeling a tad deflated. But neither of us went in for pity parties and pulling ourselves together, we'd decided to start afresh. Moving forward, Leo's job was to arrange a visit to our second-choice venue, while mine was to deal with the dress fiasco.

"So we both know what we're doing?" Leo asked, as he pulled on his jacket.

"We do."

He tapped his jeans' pocket. "I've got my phone, so I'll make an appointment over lunch."

I nodded to the laptop that sat ready and waiting on the dining table. "You can see how my morning's gonna be spent."

Leo grabbed his car keys off the hook, before kissing my cheek. "You'll find what you're looking for," he said, confident. "I have every faith." He turned to Otis. "Come on, boy. Time to go to work."

I smiled as the dog chased after him, before diverting my attention to the matter at hand. Keen to get started, I quickly made a cup of coffee and headed for the computer. Diving straight into Google, I typed in what I was looking for and as the search screen sprang to life, I took a deep breath. Such was my determination not to wear Mum's Diana affair, I was prepared to sit there all day seeking out the dress of my dreams if I had to.

Staring at image after image, I frowned. Every wedding gown available looked flamboyant and intricate, and thanks to Mum, I already had that. I realised if I was to get anywhere, I had to narrow things down, and deciding to be more specific, I keyed into the search bar every word I could think of to describe my perfect dress. I clicked enter and my face lit up as the results suddenly appeared. "Now we're talking," I said, taking in the simpler designs.

After scrolling through yet more pages, my initial delight proved misplaced. None of the dresses on offer truly matched what I'd been looking for and as frustration kicked in, I growled, half tempted to toss the laptop out of the window. "How hard can this be?"

I clicked on the cross in the corner of the screen and shut my search down altogether. Throwing myself back in my chair, it was clear I'd have to come up with a different solution. Sitting in the silence, my mind raced, a smile gradually forming on my lips, as inspiration finally struck. "That's it!" I said, leaping forward to reopen the app. "Tess, you're a genius."

Re-enthused, I set about a whole new quest. Just like earlier, I refused to be deterred and after a job well done, relief swept over me. I smiled as I clicked the screen's *place order* button. "Dress dilemma sorted."

My stomach rumbled and checking the clock, I couldn't believe how quickly the hours had passed. The time suck had ultimately been worth it though and I decided to celebrate with a well-earned late lunch. Rising to my feet I stretched out my back, before heading straight for the fridge to grab a block of cheese, a bag of rocket, and some butter.

I retrieved a loaf from the bread bin, before making the

thickest of sandwiches. I took a huge bite, appeasing my hunger, as I savoured the cheddar-licious gorgeousness. "Now for coffee," I said, ready for a much-needed caffeine hit.

Halfway through making it, I paused, my eyes narrowing at the sight of Leo's lunch pack and flask that sat on the counter. Aware that it was way past noon, I knew after a morning's hard graft the poor man had to be starving. Deciding I could eat as I drove, I glanced around for my bag, stuffed Leo's fare inside, and taking my sandwich with me, made my way out to the car.

Driving along in my battered old runaround, I was reminded of how quickly the months had gone by. It didn't seem that long ago that the dormancy of winter was at its peak, when everything and everyone, including me, hunkered down.

Glancing around, what once appeared dismal and grey, was vibrant and clement. Sheep munched on lush green grass, while their fast-growing offspring danced and played nearby. Looking at the size of the so-called babies, even lambing season was almost over. I smiled to myself, comforted in the knowledge that while time was, indeed, moving on, we still had a few months to put our wedding plans in place.

I spotted Leo's van in front of an old farmhouse and pulling up behind, I turned off the engine and unclipped my seat belt. I looked over at the property with its pale blue wooden porch, and blossoming wisteria pendants that spanned the stonework. There was no denying the presence of the woman who busied herself cutting blooms from the well-stocked flower bed that edged the front lawn.

Wearing a colourful kaftan and a scarlet red turban, she clearly had both style and confidence. Two things that I, unfortunately, lacked. Much to my shame, I had to admit that when Leo had first mentioned his elderly clients, a whole different image had sprung to mind and looking down at my jeans and T-shirt, I wished I'd thought to change before setting out.

Pruners in hand, the woman placed her cuttings into the trug basket that lay by her feet and as I climbed out of the car and slammed its door behind me, she stopped what she was doing. She looked my way as I headed up the path to introduce myself, giving me a welcoming smile as bright as her outfit.

"Sorry to interrupt," I said. "But I'm–"

"Tess?" The laughter lines around the woman's eyes deepened as her smile grew wider.

"Yes," I said, surprised she'd know that.

"Don't worry. I'm not psychic. I recognised you from Leo's description. You're exactly as he said."

I felt myself blush. Again comparing her stunning outfit to my rather scruffy choice of clothing, there was no telling if she'd meant that as a compliment or not. "He forgot these." I dug into my bag and pulled out Leo's lunch box and flask.

"Oh, sweetie, you've just missed him. He, Otis, and Hugo have gone on a mission." She frowned. "They said they were off to get more gardening supplies, but now I'm not so sure." She indicated my wares. "I wouldn't be surprised if they've snuck off for a bacon sandwich." She laughed. "The number of times that husband of mine has gone against doctor's orders."

I looked back at the woman, not sure how to respond.

"Hugo's meant to be following a strict health regime. Cutting out all the bad stuff he claims he can't live without."

"I see." I might not have said it, but Hugo sounded like my kind of chap.

The woman's expression softened. "Hark at me wittering on. I haven't even introduced myself." She put down her pruning shears and stepped forward to shake my hand. "I'm Marianne."

"Pleased to meet you." I stuffed Leo's lunch back into my bag and accepted the gesture.

"Can I offer you a cup of tea? Coffee?" She raised her eyebrows. "Something a little more exciting? After all, it's five o'clock somewhere."

Deciding I liked Marianne, I chuckled. "Why not? A coffee would be lovely."

Marianne let out a disappointed sigh, enough to tell me she'd hoped I'd choose something alcoholic. "Spoilsport." Picking up her trug, she led the way round to the back of the house which opened out onto a large flat field, more than a garden. Tonne bags of boulders sat next to mounds of gravel and winding trenches had been dug. Bags of sand and cement sat next to a concrete mixer.

With some serious landscaping going on, Leo certainly had his work cut out. Marianne placed her basket of flowers onto the outdoor table. "Shall we?" Marianne said, indicating we go inside.

Following her in, my eyes lit up. I'd never seen such a cheerful kitchen. The cupboards were painted a citrus yellow and the walls a cornflower blue. A pine dresser displayed bold floral crockery and a glass vase of pink roses sat in the centre of the circular dining table.

"Sugar?" Marianne asked, as she set about organising the coffee.

"No, thank you." My eyes were drawn to an oversized framed photo that dominated the wall above an ancient-looking chest of drawers and I moved to take a closer look. It was a work scene that showed Marianne stood at a ginormous table. Holding a pair of long-bladed scissors, she and a colleague were both laughing at something.

Convinced I recognised the second individual, I leaned in. *Surely not? It can't be.* My eyes narrowed as they flitted from the Marianne in the picture, to the Marianne in the room, and back again. "Isn't that…?" I said of her associate. Suddenly, not only did my host's attire and home décor choices make sense, I realised that me turning up at the farmhouse that day had to be providence; a sign I'd made the right decision that morning.

Marianne appeared at my side. "Zane Rafferty? It certainly is." Beaming, her expression was loaded with affection. "He was a brilliant man. A real artist. Not surprising when he took inspiration from the likes of Dutch painter Piet Montrian." Marianne handed me my drink, and taking a sip of her own, admired the picture with me for a moment.

Zane Rafferty was a world-renowned fashion designer. The rich and famous adored his creations. Taken too soon, I recalled the global shockwave following his death. There was a massive outpouring amongst celebrities. Even royalty attended his funeral.

I remembered how Sal, also a big fan of his, had been so distraught she'd cried for a week. Growing up, she idolised the man. Not for his clothes. She thought them far too whacky. It was Zane Rafferty's looks that Sal fell for. As far as my sister was concerned, he was the best-looking man on the planet. Tall, dark, and edgy, he had a fierceness in his eyes and the perfect chiselled jaw. Zane Rafferty could have hit the catwalk himself if he'd wanted to.

"I was his chief pattern maker."

"Wow," I said, impressed.

"I drafted his sketches. Translated them into patterns so his clothes could be brought to life."

"I bet that wasn't easy!" I said, recalling some of his lines.

Marianne let out a laugh, while I felt my cheeks redden, knowing I shouldn't have spoken that out loud.

"Not always. His outfits could be a bit out there."

"Looks like the two of you worked well together though," I said, indicating the laughter in the photo. "You seem to be having fun."

"We had a great relationship. Come on." Marianne gestured to the table. "I can tell you a couple of stories, if you'd like?"

A picture of Sal popped into my head. "Yes, please." Eagerly heading for a seat, I pictured my sister's face when I next caught up with her. Sal was going to be so shocked when I told her who I'd been chatting to.

CHAPTER 21

I breezed into the kitchen, ready to embrace the new day. "Good morning," I said. Heading straight for Leo, I kissed his cheek. "Anything I can do to help?"

"You seem chirpy," Leo said, handing me a rack of toast.

"Do I?" I took a seat at the table and wearing a knowing expression, reached for a knife to butter myself a slice.

Leo eyed me, suspicious, as he joined me with a plate of sausages. "A bit too chirpy."

"I didn't know there was such a thing." Picking up my fork, I helped myself to a couple of juicy pork and apples.

"There is when we've yet to find a suitable wedding location."

That hadn't been for the want of trying. Having previously telephoned our second and third choices of venue, only to be told they were already booked out, Leo and I had spent most of the previous evening trawling the internet for yet more viable options. We'd discussed a couple of places, but with one giving off too many corporate vibes and the other stretching our budget a little too much, the search was ongoing.

Despite refusing to let our lack of progress ruin my good humour, Wendy, the wedding planner, popped into my head. She reminded me that without a venue we couldn't submit our notice of intention to marry. *No notification, no wedding,* she'd said. However, I ignored her condescending tone and smug expression. "We'll find somewhere," I replied, choosing to remain positive.

"And you still haven't sorted out your dress," Leo said, as he tucked into his food.

I gave him a coy smile. "Who says I haven't?"

Leo looked at me, intrigued. "Meaning?"

I'd been hoping to surprise Leo with my ingenuity and creative thinking, but taking in his curiosity, I knew I couldn't keep things to myself any longer. I opened my mouth to speak, but a knock at the front door sounded. I froze in excitement. It seemed an explanation was no longer necessary. Instead of telling Leo what I was up to, I could show him.

I squealed as I jumped out of my seat and leaving Leo eating his breakfast, I raced out into the hall to answer. I giggled at the sight of the man standing there with the response to my prayers. "You don't know how happy I am to see you," I said.

"Something special, is it?" he asked, placing a big brown box on the ground next to my feet.

"You could say that." I clapped my hands together in delight.

The chap pulled out his mobile and took a photo of my delivery to prove that it had landed safe and sound. Picking up the box again, he handed it over. "There you go, love," he said. "Enjoy your day."

"You too." I kicked the door shut with my foot and continuing to smile, made my way back to the kitchen.

"Anyone would think it's Christmas morning," Leo said, taking in my enthusiasm. "What've you got there?"

"You'll see." I set the box down on the table and ready to reveal the solution to my wedding dress dilemma, cleared away our breakfast things to make room. I grabbed a pair of scissors from a drawer, before using them to carefully slice through the packing tape. I took a deep breath and slowly folded back the cardboard flaps. "You ready?"

Leo watched on, bemused, as I produced a pack of white cotton reels, followed by a pair of fabric shears.

"Now for the pièce de résistance," I said. Relishing the moment, I carefully lifted out the object of my glee. Another grin spread across my face. "What do you think?"

"That you've bought yourself a sewing machine?" Leo said.

"Oh, it's a lot more than that, Leo." I ran my hand over the top of it. "Thanks to this little beauty, I'll be walking down the aisle in the dress of my dreams. Not the monstrosity that Mum calls a wedding gown."

Leo furrowed his brow. "Surely, you're not thinking of..."

"Yes, Leo. That's exactly what I'm thinking." I removed every trace of protective polystyrene to admire the machine it in all its glory. "Do you know how many hours I spent on the internet yesterday poring over dresses and, as it turned out, for nothing?" I looked at Leo direct. "That's when it hit me. If I can't buy what I want, why not make it?"

"And you have the required sewing experience needed for that?" he asked, my confidence clearly doing nothing to ease his mind.

"Nope."

"So you don't actually know how to use this?" He indicated my new purchase.

I pulled out the thick instruction manual. "I will once I've read this."

Leo stared at me in much the same way that Marianne had done when I'd outlined my plan to her. It seemed they both thought I'd gone mad. "Tess, are you sure this is the route you want to take?" Leo said.

"Of course I'm sure. I mean, how hard can sewing be?"

"Maybe more difficult than you're imagining?"

I frowned at the man, wondering why he wasn't pleased for me. "Leo, you're not talking to your typical newbie here."

"But I thought you just said…"

"In case you've forgotten, I am a potter."

Leo cocked his head, evidently struggling to see the connection.

I chuckled at the man's confusion. "It means I have a head start."

Leo still didn't appear to follow.

"Not only am I used to controlling speed with one of these…" I pulled the machine's foot pedal out of the box. "Operating a wheel to manipulate clay can't be all that different to controlling fabric."

Leo seemed more amused than convinced by my reasoning.

"Obviously, I'm not going to dive straight in," I said, excited at the prospect.

"Obviously."

"I'll dig out an old bedding sheet. You know, to do a few practice runs first."

"Of course."

"Then once I've learnt all the stitches this machine can do…"

"You'll have those licked in no time," Leo said.

"There'll be no stopping me."

"There won't."

I narrowed my eyes. "You're laughing at me, aren't you?"

Leo tried to keep a straight face. "Not at all. I love the fact that you're so confident."

"You don't think I can do this."

"Well…"

"Well, nothing." I prodded him in the arm. "Oh, ye of little faith."

Leo got up from his seat. "I'm sorry." Chuckling, he leaned down and kissed my cheek. "Like you say, with a bit of practice, I'm sure you'll make a wonderful seamstress." Continuing to smile, Leo shook his head as he collected his packed lunch and flask off the kitchen counter. He laughed some more as he reached for a slice of toast to eat on his way to work. "I can't wait to see what you come up with." He turned his attention to the dog. "Otis, time to go."

I pulled the hair bobble that was wrapped around my wrist free and used it to neatly secure my hair in place ready to start. "Come tonight, you'll be eating your words," I called out, as Leo and Otis left the room and headed for the front door.

CHAPTER 22

$\mathcal{I}$ sat at the table staring at the sewing machine. With its pictured stitch dial, numbered tension dial, and basic reverse button, it might have looked simple enough to use, but images could be deceiving. No matter its appearance, or what the instruction manual said, it was not a machine for beginners.

I knew I looked as frazzled as I felt, but I was determined not to be beaten. I ran my hand through my hair for the thousandth time and as my bobble fell from my head and bounced off my shoulder, prepared to thread the tiny-eyed needle for what had to be the millionth time. I put the end of the cotton between my lips to straighten it and taking a deep breath, leant forward and took aim. Squinting, my tongue poked out of the corner of my mouth, while the strand went left, then right, and then left again.

My vision blurred as I turned cross-eyed, forcing me to blink until I could see. Realising it was time to give up, I sighed and threw myself back in my seat. I pinched the bridge of my nose. "Tell me again who said this was a good idea," I said. What was once the highly anticipated answer to my prayers, seemed to be anything but.

I thought back to that morning when I'd bragged to Leo about having a head start because I was a potter. It seemed my experience with a foot pedal and clay meant nothing when it came to working with material. Not only did the fabric want to do its own thing, when I did manage to get it moving, I found sewing in a straight line nigh on impossible. I filled my cheeks with air and exhaled, able to hear the teasing I had coming my way. Leo wouldn't be able to help himself and who could blame him?

Remembering he wasn't the only one with whom I'd outlined my plan, humiliation washed over me as I recalled the exchange I'd had with Marianne; not just a sewer, but a bona fide expert who'd worked with none other than Zane Rafferty. Marianne might have been polite to my face when I'd discussed making my own wedding dress, but she had to have been secretly laughing at my naivety. It was no wonder the woman had looked at me like I was bonkers. I continued to cringe. Thanks to my misplaced confidence, I wouldn't ever be able to face Marianne again.

The front door sounded as it opened and closed. Looking over at the clock, I was surprised to find it had gone 6pm. It appeared time flew if there was fun to be had or not. I'd at least hoped to tidy up before Leo got back.

"So how's my little seamstress getting on?" Leo asked as he and Otis entered. Leo's accompanying smile froze as he surveyed the kitchen and dining area.

"Not as well as expected," I said. With no choice but to admit my failing, I took in the massacred bedsheets that covered the chairs, half the table, and most of the floor. "As you can see, I'm not cut out for sewing."

"Oh, come on. Things can't be that bad."

My eyes went from Leo to the mess, and back again. "That's a joke, right?"

Leo joined me at the table and sitting at my side, picked up a sample of my work. He assessed the quality of my stitching. "Look at this. You've created a fantastic wave-line."

I raised my eyebrows. The man evidently knew less than I did on the sewing front. "It's meant to be straight."

"Well, what about this one?" Picking up another piece of material, I could see Leo wished he hadn't. Frowning at the hot mess of gathered fabric and knotted cotton, he appeared lost for words.

"The tension was too tight."

"And the fact that you know that shows you're learning," he replied, ever the optimist.

I sighed. "Doesn't feel that way."

"It's like you said this morning, you need a bit of practice. To develop your sewing skills."

I took the piece of material from him and tossed it to one side. "There's no point. I'm rubbish at it." Again, I took in the carnage around me. Forced to concede defeat, dressmaking was way beyond my skill set. "What am I going to do, Leo? I'd set my heart on that dress. And no way can I wear Mum's offering."

Leo rose, pulling me up with him. "You're going to let me run you a bath and while you're enjoying a long relaxing soak…" He wrapped both his hands around my waist. "I'll tidy this lot away and get started on dinner."

"That doesn't solve the problem though, does it?"

"I'm sure between us we'll come up with something. Maybe you could enrol on a sewing class? Or find some YouTube tutorials to get you properly started?"

I looked at Leo, confused by his response. "Don't you find it hard being this nice all the time?"

"What do you mean?"

"After this morning's conversation, if things were the other way around I'd be…"

"Oh, I know exactly how you'd be. But I also know how important this is to you."

The man had the understanding of a saint.

"Don't get me wrong, the teasing will come," Leo said, with a glint in his eye. "You know, a bit down the line. When your dress is less of an issue."

I chuckled, surprisingly glad to hear it.

Leo smiled. "In the meantime, how are you at darning socks?" he asked, before dodging out of harm's way.

CHAPTER 23

"I can't find my bag," I said, making a show of looking for it.

Glancing around the living room, Leo clocked the strap poking out from behind a cushion on the sofa. Pulling it free, he let it dangle from his fingers, as he turned to me with a wry smile.

"How did that get there?" I asked.

"How, indeed?" Not for the first time that morning, the man saw straight through me.

From making it clear I'd rather stay home, to insisting I had a migraine, I'd done my best to get out of going to the Cavendish family get-together. However, Leo loved our clan meetings, and much to my consternation, he'd dismissed every one of my complaints. To the point that delaying the inevitable was all I'd had left.

"Now can we go?" Leo checked his watch. "If we move fast, we might even get there on time."

Still reeling over the sewing machine debacle, I'd yet to come up with a workable solution and the last thing I wanted was to spend hours listening to Mum go on about how she couldn't wait to see me walk down the aisle in her wedding dress. I couldn't trust myself not to tell her I'd stuffed it under my bed, where it had lain there ever since, like some fabric bogey man, turning my dreams into nightmares.

Moving towards the living room door, Leo stopped and turned. "Tess, do you want to tell me what's going on?"

Even if I tried to explain, I knew Leo wouldn't get it. Every time I took issue with Mum, no matter what line she crossed, Leo considered her actions sweet and thoughtful. In comparison, my constant grievances of late made me look heartless and ungrateful. In my mind it was better to avoid Mum altogether, instead of always looking like the bad guy.

Leo raised an eyebrow. "Well, we both know there's nothing wrong with your head. As for hiding this..." he gestured to my bag.

I knew my behaviour was pathetic. But as soon as Sal had rung to let us know we were gathering at her house instead of Mum and Dad's, my brain had gone into overdrive. Especially after she'd refused to divulge why. When it came to our wedding plans, I'd already had one surprise too many. "It's nothing," I said, ready to leave the room too. "You'll just tell me I'm being soft."

Leo's expression relaxed. "Try me." Taking my hand, he led me towards the sofa. Pulling me down next to him, he gave me a sympathetic smile. "You talk, I'll listen. No judgement."

Resting my hands on my lap, I fiddled with my fingers. "Isn't it obvious?"

With nothing else left in my toolbox and a husband-to-be that was so relaxed about mum's approach to our wedding he was horizontal, I decided to play the guilt card. "You've been so busy at work, it's like you've forgotten we're meant to be getting married. And now you finally have a day off, I can't help thinking we should be doing something more productive." Lifting my gaze, I gave him my best puppy dog eyes. "Up to now, all we've sorted is a date. September's going to be here before we know it."

Leo looked back at me, deadpan. "You're worried we won't be organised in time?"

I nodded.

"Because of me?"

I nodded again.

"This from a woman who keeps telling me there's no need to panic just yet, we've got plenty of time?"

I shifted in my seat. "Yes."

"Okay." He twisted round to face me head on. "Now tell me what's really happening here."

I narrowed my eyes, frustrated that I wasn't a better actor. I sighed. "If you must know, I'm worried about lots of things."

"Such as?"

"The change in the get-together rota, for one." No way would Mum give up her spot unless something was afoot.

"But that's a good thing, isn't it? I thought you'd be pleased."

I envisaged all the Cavendishes sat round Mum's dining table, working through our cutlery, as course after course appeared in front of us. I might love Mum's food, but her turns to host were far too formal and my belly hurt just thinking about them. I couldn't deny that out of the two, an afternoon at my sister's was preferable.

"Don't get me wrong, I love going to Sal's," I said. "But I'm worried about what we're walking into because we both know Mum wouldn't agree to this without good reason. I've had enough shockers to deal with, what with mood boards, wedding planners and whatnot, I don't think I can take any more." I felt my blood pressure rising. "And to be honest, I'm dreading seeing Mum."

"I don't see why. I mean, I know she's been a bit full-on, but that's only because she cares."

"Because I haven't a clue what I'm going to say when she brings up that bloody dress. And she will. She won't be able to help herself." I pictured its puffy sleeves, embroidered heart motif, and endless train. "She's going to freak when I say I'm not wearing it."

"If that's all that's worrying you, the answer's simple."

Not to me it wasn't.

"Don't tell her. At least, not yet."

I couldn't believe he thought the solution to my dilemma was that simple. Leo clearly hadn't learnt anything from Mum's behaviour those last weeks. "That won't stop her, she'll still go on. I can already hear her constant wittering about how beautiful I'm going to look. As will our daughter, and no doubt, our granddaughter." I knew I was rambling, but it was one of those *I've started, so I'll finish* moments. "You do know she's decided it's an heirloom. To pass on, generation after generation. If there's ever a time to pray for a male-only bloodline, it's now."

Leo chuckled. "It can't be that bad."

"Honestly, it's awful." I sighed. "I'm so fed up with all the pushing back, Leo. I wish the woman would listen once and for all."

"Come on." Leo rose to his feet. "It's time I saw this dress for myself."

"Why?" I asked, refusing to move. "So you can tell me I'm overreacting. That there's nothing wrong with it. It's only another example of what a saint my mother is."

Leo shook his head with a smile, before sitting again. "I know it might seem like I'm always taking your Mum's side, Tess. But just because Patricia can be a bit barmy sometimes, that doesn't mean her heart isn't in the right place."

I knew Leo was right. Mum's behaviour might be a bit controlling, but she wasn't malicious or cruel. Even if making me wear that damn dress felt it.

Leo smiled. "You two are more alike than you care to admit."

I scowled, affronted by the mere suggestion. "I'm nothing like my mother."

"Really? I bet Patricia's had a few headaches when she doesn't want to go somewhere too."

Thinking about my morning's behaviour, I supposed we Cavendishes were all a tad eccentric. However, in my opinion, Mum took things to another level. Once she'd made up her mind about something, there was no going back. I scoffed. Even when it came to her daughter's wedding.

Leo stood up again. "Now, let's go see that dress."

"We can't."

"Why not?"

"What do you mean, why not?" I was surprised he had to ask. "Because it's bad luck."

"Only if you wear it."

He had a point. "Like that's gonna happen."

"So what's the problem?" Leo hoisted me back onto my feet and nodded towards the doorway. "It's only fair I see what all the fuss is about."

Leading the way, I headed upstairs to the bedroom. I pointed to its hiding place under the bed.

Leo got down on his knees and reaching out, he grimaced as he wrangled with the garment bag. Pulling it into view, he groaned as he picked it up and hung it on the wardrobe door. "Why is it so heavy?"

I undid the zip, and a mountain of fabric immediately spilled out. "That's why," I said.

"Jesus Christ."

Freeing the dress altogether, I turned to Leo who stood there, wide-eyed and speechless. "Don't say I didn't warn you."

Leo swallowed, as if trying and failing to find the right words. At last, he opened his mouth to speak. "I'll never doubt your word again."

"Doubt me? You mean you thought I was exaggerating?"

"Well, yes. Never in my wildest dreams did I think a mother

would do this…" He indicated the wedding gown. "…to their daughter."

"And now you know mine would!"

"Sorry, Tess. No wonder you've been panicking."

Finally, we were on the same page.

As he continued to stare at the dress, his eyes grew wider. "Isn't that…? It looks just like…"

"Princess Diana's affair?" I said, before he could finish.

"Bloody hell, Tess." He let out a snigger. "You definitely can't wear it, you'll be the laughing stock."

"Going off your and Sal's reactions, I already am. As for Chloe and Abbey's reaction. They're still sending funny pictures through."

"I mean, it's horrific."

"Which is exactly what I've been telling you."

Mesmerised, Leo took a step closer. "I can't believe your mum actually wore this herself. Even back in the day." Lifting his hand to touch it, he smiled as he stroked the material. "To be fair, it feels better than it looks. Which I suppose is something."

"Never mind that." I tapped his hand back down. "What am I going to do?"

"Get another dress."

I stared at him. Talk about stating the obvious. "And in the meantime? When it comes to Mum?"

"If she does bring it up…"

"There's no *if* about it."

"Then I'll have to deal with it."

"And how do you plan on doing that?"

"Don't worry. I'll think of something."

CHAPTER 24

"*H*ere she is," Ryan said, calling out from the kitchen doorway. "The latest royal in the family."

I rolled my eyes as Leo and I hung our coats on the banister. Having just landed at Sal's I'd expected some quip or other. My brother-in-law couldn't help himself. "You've seen the photo then?" I asked, as we approached.

Ryan chuckled. "Oh yes."

"There's a picture?" Leo asked. "Of you wearing your mother's dress?" He looked to Ryan with a mischievous smile. "Mate, you've got to send it to me."

"You'll do nothing of the sort," I said.

Leo chuckled as we made our way down the hall. "But think of the children, Tess."

I tried to keep a straight face. "Forget it. We have enough pictures on the mantelpiece."

Entering the room, I stopped. "What's all this?" Taking in the sight before me, I'd never felt so relieved. It seemed I'd been wrong to worry about potential surprises; some of them turned out to be pretty good. My eyes followed the line of delicious-looking cakes that sat on the countertop next to two glasses of water. "Someone's been busy."

"I know we should all be at Mum and Dad's this month," Sal said. "I just thought we could use the afternoon to do a tasting session. You know, decide what flavour you want for the big day."

I looked to Leo. "Did you know about this?"

Leo shook his head.

"A bit early, isn't it?" I asked. With three months to go, I assumed we had loads of time for that kind of decision.

"You think? September will be here before you know it."

India caught my attention when she strode, one hand on hip, into the room.

Usually one for nerd chic, my niece couldn't have dressed more differently. She wore a dusty green ruffle maxi dress, which she'd teamed with a pair of pink-suede gum-soled hushpuppies. She stopped just in front of me, and raising her oversized rectangle sunglasses to scan my choice of attire, looked me up and down. Full of disdain, she shook her head at my worn jeans and fitted black T-shirt, before continuing further into the room.

"Fashion model?" I said to Sal.

My sister nodded. "After the gerbil affair, we thought it best to move on."

"She got the idea from you two actually," Ryan said.

"Us?" Going off my wardrobe, I couldn't believe that.

"It's to do with being your bridesmaid," Sal said, as if reading my mind.

India came to a second halt. This time next to Leo. "I've been practising my walk," she said.

"For when you stroll down the aisle?" he asked.

India smiled. "Aisle, runway. Tom-ay-to, tom-ah-to."

Great, I thought. On top of everything else, an eleven-year-old girl planned to upstage me.

India turned with a flourish. "Later," she said, swanning back out of the room.

A picture of Marianne popped into my head. "Talking of

fashion," I said, suddenly animated. "You'll never guess who Leo's working for?"

"One of Ed's friends, isn't it?" Ryan said.

"I didn't even know Dad had any," Sal said. She shrugged in answer to my question. "One of his new golfing buddies?"

Ryan let out a laugh. "That's got to be an exercise thing. As far as I'm aware, your father doesn't like watching golf, never mind playing it."

"Forget Dad," I said. "Sal, do you remember Zane Rafferty?"

My sister swooned at the mention of his name. "Do I."

Ryan appeared mystified. "Never heard of him." He looked from Sal to me. "Should I have? Who is he?"

"Only the most handsome man that ever lived," Sal replied.

Ryan rolled his eyes. "Present company excepted, of course. Eh, Leo?"

"Leo's working for his chief pattern maker," I carried on. "The woman who turned his creations from a sketch into a blueprint, which was then used to make his clothes for real."

"Really?" Shock spread across Sal's face.

Giggling at her response, I knew she'd be impressed.

"Where did Dad meet *her*?" Sal asked.

"He's actually friends with Hugo, Marianne's husband," Leo said.

"Going off your two's chatter I'm guessing this woman and her husband are important," Ryan said. "And they do say golf is the sport of kings."

"I thought that was hunting," I said.

Ryan snickered. "You'd know. You being royalty and all that."

While I nudged Ryan for his cheek, my sister sighed. "Zane Rafferty. I loved that man. I was convinced I was going to marry him. Then he had to go and die on me."

"I thought you didn't believe in marriage?" Leo asked.

"For him, I'd have done anything."

Ryan shook his head at Sal. "Time to get back in the real world, love." He indicated the kitchen countertop. "We've got a shedload of cakes to taste here."

Leo laughed. "Ready when you are."

Ryan picked up two forks. Handing one to Leo, he kept the other for himself.

"I'll take that." Sal snatched Ryan's away.

"What are you doing?" he asked.

She handed it to me. "You..." my sister said to Ryan. "Can wait for the leftovers."

Ryan tutted at the unfairness. "Bet you wouldn't say that to Zane *whatshisname*."

"Damn right I wouldn't." Sal gave him a mock stern look. "Shouldn't you be off collecting dinner?"

"Why?" He gestured to the various cakes on offer. "No one's going to be hungry after eating this lot."

Sal's stare continued.

"Okay, okay." Ryan put his hands up in defeat, before grabbing his keys from the table. As he headed out to leave, he paused and bowed his head in my direction. "Your majesty."

"Go!" Sal said, laughing.

With her husband out of the way, she indicated the first cake. "Shall we get started?" she said, coming over all professional.

We didn't need asking twice. Leo and I dug straight in.

"This one's lemon and elderflower, known for being fragrant and refreshing."

It seemed it was my turn to swoon. "With a light and delicate texture," I said, going in for another mouthful.

"I like," Leo said. "Sal, you're a baking genius."

Much to my disappointment, Sal indicated the glasses of water for us to drink from. As we moved on to our next sample, I could easily have loitered on the first. "This one is vanilla and raspberry," my sister said. "The sweetness of one should complement the sharpness of the other."

I took in the plump fruit that had been mixed into the sponge and eagerly stuffing it into my mouth, I couldn't help but close my eyes while I chewed. "Oh, it does. And it's so moist."

"Tastes like summertime," Leo said, smiling as we both dove in for seconds.

Again, Sal gestured to the water. "The next one is a white chiffon cake."

"It is pale, isn't it?" I said, putting a forkful into my mouth. "Ooh, it's very light."

Leo's shoulders dropped. "It's like a fluffy cloud melting in my mouth."

"High praise, indeed," Sal said, chuckling as she, once again, forced Leo and me to cleanse our palette. "Now on to the richer two. Starting with a chocolate cake."

As soon as it hit my tongue, I knew I was in chocolatey heaven. "So creamy."

"Definitely denser than the others," Leo said.

"And finally…" Sal waited for us to finish our next round of water. "We have a traditional fruit cake."

"Last but not least," I said, digging in for the final time.

"And the fruit, by the way, has been soaked in the finest brandy I could get."

I winced. "You can say that again."

"This one reminds me of Christmas," Leo said.

"Now I can make some alternatives if none of them fit the bill."

I looked at my sister, incredulous. "These are great," I said. "I'd choose them all if I could."

"I agree," Leo said. "Except for the last one. It's a bit yuletide for me."

"Do you prefer any of them in particular?" Sal asked.

"I think we need to try them all again," I said. "You know, to be sure."

Fork at the ready, Leo nodded his agreement.

"Yoo hoo!" Mum called out, as Leo and I were about start our second run.

My face fell. Just like that, the fun was over.

$\mathcal{M}$um breezed into the room with Dad close behind. "How is everyone?" Mum's smile froze. "What's all this?" She gestured toward the forks in my and Leo's hands.

"Cake sampling," Sal said. "They're trying to decide which flavour they want for the wedding."

Mum's gaze went from Sal to me. "Without us?"

Dad shook his head. "Why did *we* need to be here?"

"It's not a case of need, Edward. I'd simply thought Leo and Tess might have wanted our opinion."

By *our* I assumed Mum meant hers.

Mum's eyes scrutinised the demolished cakes. "Looks like someone's had more than a taste." She turned her attention to me. "Tess, shouldn't you be watching your weight? The last thing you want is to have to alter your wedding gown."

"Patricia!" Dad said.

"What?" Mum frowned at him. "I didn't mean it like that." She rolled her eyes, as she looked my way again. "No dieting either, young lady. A few pounds either way could ruin the fit."

Her comment came as no surprise. Mum had never accepted my ability to eat as little or as much as I wanted without either affecting my weight. However, even less surprising was the fact that it had taken Mum all of sixty seconds to bring up that damned dress.

"Tea, anyone? Coffee?" Sal trained her eyes on me. "Something stronger?"

"I'll help," Dad said. As he headed to put the kettle on, my sister pulled out a bottle of wine from the fridge. "Where's Ryan?" Dad asked.

As the two of them began making small talk about Ryan's whereabouts, Mum watched on.

"How are things progressing with the invites, Patricia?" Leo said.

Too busy observing Dad and Sal, Mum didn't seem to hear.

"Patricia?" Leo said, raising his voice a little.

As she turned her attention back to me and Leo, her eye appeared to twitch, but as quickly as it appeared the tic was gone. "Oh, yes." Mum, at last, focused. "I'm glad you asked." She headed for the dining table, and plonking her handbag down, reached inside. "I've brought one to show you." She smiled. "I hope you're ready for this?" she said, pulling out what appeared to be a gold envelope. Handing it over for us to have a closer look, she excitedly awaited our response.

The woman was clearly running with the royal theme, as the flap was laser-cut into an ornate crown design. Rather than being the envelope I'd thought it was, the whole thing opened out to reveal a pop-up silhouetted bride and groom. Appearing to look into each other's eyes, they stood on what looked like a stage, while a chandelier dangled above their heads.

"You see those pockets?" Mum said, indicating yet more fancy laser-cut sections. "The invitation goes in one, and the RSVP in the other."

"That's some creation," Leo said, while I mouthed *What the...?* behind my mother's back. Clamping down on his lips, Leo did his best not to react.

"Isn't it," Mum replied, taking Leo's words as a compliment. "Obviously, we need to talk venues. I mean, have we organised one yet?"

I winced. There was the word *we* again.

"Because I can't send these out if I don't know where the ceremony's taking place?"

"We loved Gregbrook Manor, didn't we, Tess?"

"We did," I replied. "It had this fabulous glass-domed orangery that led out onto the perfect courtyard, complete with French fountain."

"A French fountain?" Mum said. "That does sound perfect." Her excitement built. "Please tell me you've booked it?"

"We were tempted. But the place is just too big," Leo said.

"Is there such a thing?" Mum asked.

"There is when you only have twenty-seven people and a dog to cater for," I replied. "Honestly, Mum, the space was huge."

"And everywhere else is either already taken or not for us," Leo continued. "But don't worry. We'll let you know as soon as we've organised somewhere."

"I understand," Mum said.

Her cogs began to turn. Wondering what was going on in that head of hers, I narrowed my eyes. Watching her, she reminded me of a supervillain devising a dastardly scheme, and not for the first time, I wished I had the power of telepathy. "Whatever it is you're thinking, Mum, forget it," I said.

Mum snapped back into the room. She fixed a smile on her face. "I don't know what you're talking about."

CHAPTER 26

$\mathcal{I}$ stood under the hot shower, trying to wake myself up. Hardly surprising, considering I'd endured the worst night's sleep imaginable. I'd spent hours tossing and turning, before finally drifting off. But thanks to a nightmare I simply couldn't escape, even then my slumber was far from restful. It didn't matter how many times I forced myself awake, I kept falling back into the same horror.

As in my earlier dream, it was the day of my wedding. But instead of being in a garden, surrounded by friends and family, I was in the bridal suite of a castle with just my mother for company. There were no luxuries to enjoy. The room was freezing and with only a bed and the four bare stone walls that surrounded us, it felt more like a prison cell. I had on Mum's awful Princess Diana wedding dress, but it must have shrunk because it was too small at the back.

Mum groaned as she pulled at the fastenings, trying to get them to meet, all the while hissing at me for not heeding her warning about my eating. When she did manage to secure everything, I couldn't breathe and putting my hand up to my chest, I was forced to take short sharp gasps to get oxygen back into my lungs.

Wheezing, I tried to explain that the dress was crushing my ribcage, but Mum didn't listen, let alone notice the pain I was in. She simply smiled and kept telling me how beautiful I looked.

I shuddered. As dreams went, there was a lot to unpack in that one.

I slammed off the water. It seemed no amount of hair-washing, soaping up, and rinsing could shake the fuzziness from my sleep-deprived brain and grabbing a towel, I stepped out of the shower, dried myself off and got dressed.

Dragging my feet as I went, I was in no mood to herald the new day, but as I headed downstairs, I hadn't even reached the bottom step when I was confronted by Leo's good humour. I frowned, as the smell of cooking and the sound of whistling floated on the air. The last thing I needed was his chirpiness. I needed silence and caffeine.

"Do you have to?" I asked, as I entered the kitchen.

Leo turned his attention to the dog. "Sounds like someone got out of the wrong side of bed this morning, eh, Otis?"

I flopped onto a chair and placing my elbows on the table, rested my chin in my hands.

Leo smiled as he plonked a plate of waffles and the desired cup of coffee in front of me.

"Sorry," I said. "I didn't mean to sound harsh." I straightened myself up and pushed the plate away.

While Otis appeared hopeful due to my lack of appetite, Leo looked at me, aghast. "Is everything okay?"

"I'm fine, why?" I picked up my drink and took a huge gulp.

"You're not sick, are you?"

I smiled. "Not at all." I drank another mouthful of coffee. "I just didn't sleep very well."

"Even so, it's not like you to decline breakfast." Leo narrowed his eyes. "This sudden lack of appetite isn't because of what Patricia said the other day, is it? About us eating too much cake."

"Honestly," I replied. "I'm just not hungry." As Leo's concern continued, I could see he didn't quite believe me. Then again, after the dream I'd had, I wasn't sure if I one hundred per cent did either.

"Tell you what." Leo sat next to me. "Why don't I take the morning off?"

"There's no need. I'm not poorly." I smiled. "But thank you for the offer."

"In that case..." Leo slid the plate of food back towards me and picking up a knife and fork, held them out for me to take. "Prove it."

I rolled my eyes. But the last thing I wanted was Leo worrying about me. I cut into my breakfast and shoved a piece of waffle into my mouth.

"That's my girl." Leo got up from his seat and kissed my cheek, before gathering up his lunch box and keys. "Time to go, Otis."

I waited until I heard Leo's van drive off before rising to my feet and happy that the coast was clear, I headed straight for the bin. Scraping my breakfast plate clean, I then dropped both it and my cutlery into the sink. I felt tempted to go back to bed, but decided against it.

With thoughts of my supervillain mum and the wedding swirling around my head, I didn't want to risk another bad dream. Rather, I glanced around the room, insisting I should do something productive. However, too tired to even try to make sense of the sewing machine or scroll page after page on the computer to try to resolve my dress issue once and for all, I instead chose to head to the one place that always brought me calm – my workshop.

CHAPTER 27

Satisfied with a job well done, I smiled as I took in the lines of pots that adorned the wall-to-wall shelves. I'd spent hours cleaning bisque-fired mugs and bowls with a damp sponge, getting rid of any dust before, tongs in hand, dipping each piece into a bucket of newly mixed glaze.

Using a ladle-like motion, this part of the ceramics process had always felt therapeutic and with something other than Mum, bad dreams, and the wedding to think about, all thoughts of the outside world had vanished.

Such was my concentration, even the painstaking task of blending leftover drip or tong marks with a cotton bud had managed to quieten my tired yet overactive brain. All that was left to do was put them in the kiln ready for their final firing.

My stomach rumbled and suddenly hungry, it seemed my appetite was back. I headed out into the garden and breathed in the warm fresh air. Summer had arrived and as I made my way to the house, I decided to enjoy my late lunch sandwich al fresco.

Just as I got to the kitchen door, the sound of a vehicle pulling up caught my attention. I turned, and wondering who it could be, was surprised to see Leo and Otis jump out of the van. Having told Leo I'd be fine without him, the last thing I wanted was him worrying about me. "Why aren't you at work?" I asked.

Leo smiled as he approached, while Otis set off wandering, nose down, around the garden. "I've arranged a few days off," Leo said.

"Why?" I frowned. "In case you've forgotten, we do have a wedding to pay for."

"Some things are more important than money. And don't worry, Hugo and Marianne are fine with it. To be honest, it's a heavy-going project and although he'd never admit it, I think Hugo's looking forward to the rest."

I envisaged all the tonne bags I'd seen when I'd gone to drop Leo's lunch off that day. "So why not let *you* get on with it?" I asked. "Isn't that what he's paying you for?"

"Because it's important to him. That garden's been a few years in the planning, and he wants to be involved."

Putting all thoughts of Hugo to one side, I got back to the matter at hand. "This sudden need for a break isn't because of earlier, is it?" I pictured Leo's concern when I pushed my plate away at breakfast. "It was one meal, Leo."

"I know. But it's not like you to skip food. And whether you admit it or not, all this stuff with your mum and your dress and whatever other hiccups we have going on, deep down, they're bound to have an impact."

Recalling the previous night's tossing and turning, I knew I'd be lying if I denied that.

"I just think we need to step back. To forget about the wedding for a short while. Then we can reassess and start again. With clear heads."

I scoffed. "Everyone else thinks we should be speeding things up."

"We're not everyone else. Which brings me to the question of…"

"Go on," I said, wondering what was coming.

Leo wrinkled his nose in anticipation. "How do you feel about taking off somewhere?"

"What do you mean, taking off?"

Leo put his hands around my waist. "Only for a couple of nights."

"It's a bit short notice," I said, surprised we were talking about going anywhere at all.

I could see Leo's mind was set, and as he willed me to agree, I felt myself relent. "You have somewhere in mind?"

Leo smiled. "As a matter of fact, I do. I spoke to Mum and Dad earlier and asked them if they fancied a couple of visitors?"

"Really?" Just the thought of meeting Leo's parents in the flesh for the first time made me nervous.

Leo nodded. "And you don't have to look so worried. They'll love you as much as I do."

I pictured the two of us, hand in hand, strolling along a vast expanse of beach, trying to keep an eye on Otis who danced and pranced at the shoreline, before racing off into the distance.

I envisaged us enjoying a pint of Guinness in a crowded pub, where everyone sang traditional Irish folk songs to the sound of fiddles, Uilleann pipes, and Bodhrán drums. More importantly, I saw Leo getting to spend time with his own mum and dad instead of mine for a change. "I'm not so sure about that," I said. "But it would be better to meet them before our actual wedding day."

"Brilliant," Leo said, smiling. He leaned in and kissed me. "I love you, Tess Cavendish."

"And I you."

Leo suddenly stepped back and eagerly indicated the house. "Come on. We need to get packing."

I laughed. "What? Now?"

"Oh, yes. We're booked on the early morning ferry from Scotland."

CHAPTER 28

*T*urning green might be a fallacy when it came to sea sickness, but as we drove off the ferry I felt like the exception to the rule. To say it had only lasted two hours, that was some crossing. Even Otis, who sat upright on the back seat, had done better than me, and he'd been stuck in the car throughout.

I knew that my growing nerves at meeting Leo's parents for the first time weren't helping, but as we left Belfast port behind, the swaying sensation of the boat refused to abate. Nausea continued to well through my body and I had to focus on not throwing up. "If this is anything like Chloe's pregnancy sickness, she has my deepest sympathy."

"It wasn't even rough," Leo said, doing his best not to laugh.

I knew he was picturing me laid flat on my back, in the centre on the inner-deck floor. But he and my fellow passengers could chuckle all they wanted. Having read somewhere that that was where a boat was at its most stable, sea sickness was worse than any embarrassment and I'd have done anything to make it stop.

"I'll be all right soon," I said. Bile rose in my throat and forced to swallow, I already dreaded the return journey. "How long before we get there?"

Leo put his hand on my knee. "A good few hours, I'm afraid."

Oh, Lordy. Just the thought of driving for that long made me want to heave. Desperate, I wound my window down and stuck my head out into the open air. My hair blew around in all directions and as the wind hit my face, my eyes began to water.

"You can't travel like that," Leo said.

"Watch me."

CHAPTER 29

Over three hours and two dog walks later, I'd finally begun to feel better.

"Good to see you smiling again," Leo said.

With all signs of modern civilisation well behind us, we travelled on the coastal road that led to Leo's parents' house. To our right, there were rugged mountains, to our left it was next stop Canada. I looked down onto mile-long beaches and wild blue seas. Waves frothed as they swept onto the sands or crashed against cliff sides. "It's hard not to smile looking at this scenery."

Leo chuckled as he glanced at the raging ocean. "You can see why they call it the Wild Atlantic Way."

I sighed. "And why your parents love it."

In one hundred metres, turn right, the satnav suddenly instructed.

"Does that mean we're here?" I asked. Straightening myself up in my seat and wishing I hadn't been forced to spend most of the journey with my head out of the window, I raised a hand to smooth down my windswept hair.

Leo flicked on his indicator, and we took a sharp right onto a narrow lane. Wide enough for just one car, we wound down towards the sea. "We certainly are," Leo replied with a smile.

As the house came into view, it looked nothing like the one Leo and his brother had talked about. Apparently, when Grace and Bill had originally purchased the property, there hadn't been much thatch left so it was basically roofless. The exterior paintwork had long faded to a dirty dull grey, while the windows and doors had been boarded up to protect the inside from the elements. Not that there had been anything to protect. After years of abandonment, the interior walls had turned green as damp and mould took hold. There was no garden as such, merely an overgrown plot.

"I can't believe this used to be a wreck," I said.

"Me neither." Leo had seen some of Grace and Bill's photographs from before works started and during. Plus, he'd had the odd tour via video call. But as we turned off the lane and pulled onto the drive next to the newly renovated garage, it was clear neither had done the place justice and Leo's face lit up as much as mine.

The roof, which appeared strong had been completely rethatched, while the house's exterior was painted a brilliant white. The window frames and hardwood porch door were a vivid red and the plot was now a proper garden with flowers beds that bloomed bright with helenium, astrantia, and verbascum.

"Oh. My. Word," I said. Best of all was the house's view – a one-hundred-and-eighty-degree vista of the Atlantic Ocean. The wind whipped my hair around my face as I climbed out of the car for a better look, but pushing it away, I didn't care. Listening to the crashing of the waves, I was entranced.

"Isn't that something," Leo said, leaving Otis on the back seat while he joined me.

I felt his arm wrap around my shoulders as we stood there for a moment, soaking up the sight and roaring sound.

"This place is incredible," Leo said.

"Stunning," I said.

"Thank the Lord, you're here!" a woman's voice called out.

We spun round to see Grace racing out of the cottage door, her arms outstretched ready to greet us. She wore scruffy baggy jeans and a loose-fitting sweater that hung lower at one side, and her long grey hair was tied up into a bun. "Leo," she said, through the biggest of smiles. Throwing herself at him, she squeezed him in a tight embrace. She, at last, stepped back to take a good look at him. "I see this young lady's been looking after you."

He smiled, before giving me a wink. "It's more like the other way around, Mum."

Turning her attention to me, Grace wrapped me in a welcoming hug. "And that's just the way it should be," she said. "It's so lovely to meet you in person at last, Tess."

"Son!" Bill appeared in the doorway. Rushing out to join us, he too encircled his arms around first Leo and then me. "It's good to finally have you here. Both of you."

"It's great to be here, Dad," Leo said. "Although I am wondering what's happened to you both?" He mock frowned at Bill's woolly hat that struggled to contain his wild grey curls. He took in his dad's paint-splattered overalls, and sturdy black boots, before turning to his mum and raising his eyebrow at her choice of dress. "It seems the house isn't the only thing around here to undergo a transformation."

I stopped myself from laughing. According to Leo, Bill was once a suited and booted kind of chap. While Grace used to have blonde hair and wore the full works when it came to make-up.

"Cheeky," Grace said. "You can't shift that lot in a pair of high heels." She pointed to a huge mound of peat that sat next to the garage we'd parked by.

"It's a different way of life out here," Bill said. "There's always work to be done."

"Worth it though," I said, looking out to sea once more.

"You can say that again," Bill said. "Beats shuttling back and forth to Leeds every day, I can tell you."

Leo had explained that before their retirement, Bill had been a city IT expert, while his mum had owned a successful hair salon.

"What about you, Grace?" I asked. "Do you miss your work?"

She indicated her surroundings. "What do you think?"

Otis whined. He bounced up and down on the back seat, prompting Leo to lift the boot lid. Otis clambered over the headrests and jumped out to freedom, while Leo pulled out our bags.

"Come on. Let's get you both settled," Bill said, ushering us inside.

Entering through the porch, I couldn't help but admire what Bill and Grace had achieved. "This is gorgeous," I said. A staircase to the right led upstairs, while the rest of the space made up Grace and Bill's main living areas. The ceilings were double height, showing off some of the original beams and the white walls, wooden window lintels, and slate floor were perfect for the old cottage.

Despite having a cosy feel, the room was open plan. An inglenook sat to the left, around which an inviting floral sofa and a couple of mismatched armchairs had been arranged. A big wooden dining table separated the lounge area from the kitchen. With its stripped pine cupboards, this was also home to a solid fuel range which I guessed was used to heat the house's cast iron radiators as well as for cooking.

"I knew you'd been busy, but this is incredible," Leo said, clearly as impressed as me.

"Your dad's been at it seven days a week since we moved here," Grace said proudly. "This is all his work, you know."

"Not quite all, love. I've had a bit of help and advice along the way."

"And we've had the support of you know who?" Grace said, her gaze flitting upward.

I waited for her to expand, but no explanation on *you know who's* identity was forthcoming.

"But still, Dad," Leo carried on. "You've got to be proud of what you've achieved. Compared to what it was, this is a whole new house. You've worked miracles."

Bill blushed. "Thank you, son. That means a lot."

"Let me show you your room," Grace said. "And once you've sorted yourselves out, we can have a proper catch-up." Leading us through a door by the stairs, we stepped into an inner hall that revealed three more internal doors. "This is the bathroom," she said, opening one.

The space was decorated in natural tones and textures. The floor, consisting of ornate black-and-white tiles, contrasted perfectly with the space's soothing sage green panelling and natural wood shelves. I swooned at the claw-foot bath, hoping I got the chance to try it out during our stay.

"There are two bedrooms to choose from, but I thought you'd prefer the one at the front because it has the sea view." Grace swung open the door for us.

My eyes widened at the sight that met us. "This is lovely."

"Now, I'll go put the kettle on," Grace said. "And maybe make us all a spot of lunch?"

As Grace closed the door behind her, Leo and I took in the small but perfectly formed bedroom. The vast ceiling height didn't extend to that side of the house, but apart from in the bathroom, the slate flooring had continued throughout. A cast iron double bed sat on a beige rug opposite the window, with simple cross-legged tables serving as bedside cabinets. The bedding was crisp and white, and while plumped-up pillows and cushions mingled at the top end, an ecru throw lay across the bottom. There was an oak wardrobe and chest of drawers, and the room's window dressing consisted of two simple sheer curtain panels.

"I love this house," I said to Leo. "I want to move in."

We both gravitated to the window, where we stood looking out at the Atlantic Ocean.

"Thank you for bringing me here," I said.

Leo put his arm around my shoulders and gave me a squeeze.

I smiled, and soaking up the view, continued to marvel at the horizon. I took a deep breath and let out a contented sigh. Leo had been right to suggest we take a step back from the wedding and despite only having a couple of days, I was determined to make the most of the peace.

CHAPTER 30

*B*y the time Leo and I had unpacked and rejoined Grace and Bill, the dining table was laid, and lunch was ready and waiting. "This looks lovely," I said, taking in the huge salad bowl and board of freshly cut bread.

"Mixed leaves, mozzarella, mint, and prosciutto," Grace said. "With a bit of peach thrown in for the fun." She indicated we all sit. "Food for the body *and* the soul."

"I can see that," I replied, as we all took seats. Having felt too sick to eat throughout the journey over, I was more than ready to dive in.

Grace gave Leo an approving look. However, while I felt pleased to have created a good impression, Leo let out a quiet chuckle, leaving me wondering what was so funny.

"Shall we?" Grace said.

Feeling ravenous, I immediately went to pick up my fork, but Grace took hold of my hand before I got to it. To my further surprise, Bill reached out for my other hand and suddenly, *everyone* was linked palm to palm. Taking things one step further, Grace bowed her head and as she closed her eyes, mine widened.

"Bless us, O Lord," Grace suddenly said.

Glancing around, I felt a tad awkward. It seemed that Grace's earlier comment had less to do with *body* and more to do with *soul*. Returning Bill's smile, I felt myself blush. I could see we were both trying to act like our holding hands within an hour of meeting each other was perfectly normal.

"And these, thy gifts that we are about to receive."

I'd never been one for religion, let alone to thank the Lord for my food, and suddenly aware that the *you know who* whom Grace had previously mentioned was none other than Jesus, the son of God, I looked to Leo, silently questioning why he hadn't thought to give me the heads-up.

"Thank you for bringing our son, Leo, home to us. Along with his beautiful fiancée."

Doubting that anyone had ever prayed for me before either, it was one thing respecting people's right to hold their faith, but another to be thrown in at the deep end. Despite his apparent lack of seriousness over the matter, Leo had never talked about his religious background and having thought I knew everything there was to know about the man, it was disconcerting to realise that wasn't the case.

"Through Christ our Lord. Amen."

"Amen," Leo and Bill said.

As Grace opened her eyes again, she indicated it was time to let go of each other. She nodded to the salad. "Go, eat your food with gladness, and drink your wine. Ecclesiastes, Chapter 9, verse 7."

Leo's amusement continued as he handed me the salad bowl.

"Thank you," I said, through gritted teeth. Realising I had no choice but to go with the flow, I followed Grace's advice and loaded my plate with food.

"So how are the wedding plans coming along?" Bill asked.

"To be honest," I replied, pretending that what just happened, hadn't really happened, "we haven't got very far."

"Really?" he said. "With September round the corner, I'd have thought you'd more or less have everything in place."

"For one, I'm having issues finding the right dress."

"Really?" Grace said.

I nodded. "And although we've made a list, we still have to contact photographers and whatnot."

"That's all fluff though, isn't it?" Grace said. "Yes, it's nice to have pictures of the day, but it's the ceremony that counts. The vows you share."

"We think so too," Leo said.

His accompanying wink melted my heart a little and I almost forgave him for not warning me about his family's religious practices.

"As long as you have a venue," Grace continued. "You're good to go."

I opened my mouth to explain the struggle we'd had finding that too, but Grace continued talking.

"And there are some wonderful churches in your area. Something we saw for ourselves, didn't we, Bill?"

"Oh, yes," he replied. "We certainly did."

While I wondered if I'd imagined the hint of sarcasm in Bill's tone, Grace appeared not to notice.

"We visited Saint Michael and All Angels, Saint Mary's, Saint Wilfred's, Saint Alkelda's..." she said.

As religious figures went, that last one was new to me.

"And the rest." Bill sighed. "That was some pilgrimage."

"Which was the one with the Norman font?" Grace asked her husband.

"Hard to say. We packed in so many."

"You know, the one with the oldest font in Europe?" Grace pondered a moment. "You must remember it, Bill. It stood at the foot of that mountain?" She continued to wrack her brains. "Oh, what was it called?"

"Saint Oswald's," I said, pleased to be able to put her out of her misery.

Grace, Bill, and Leo froze, each with their forks midway to their mouths.

I looked back at them, pleased they all appreciated my input. I might not be religious, but that didn't mean I couldn't enjoy old buildings. "It's a lovely little church, rich in history and architecture," I said, between eating. "It dates back to the early eleven hundreds. Probably during the reign of Henry I or possibly Stephen. Although if I remember rightly the surviving parish records only go back to 1556."

Grace put her fork down. "Did you hear that, you two?"

"We certainly did," they both said.

"And you're right, Grace, the font *is* beautiful," I carried on. "Tub-shaped with a herringbone decoration." All stuff I'd learned way back when in history class at school, not once did I ever think I'd need it.

Leo and Bill stared at me, as if questioning my sanity.

"What?" I asked, wondering what I'd said wrong.

Grace, however, couldn't have been more delighted. She put down her fork, reached over and put a hand on my arm. "I knew as soon as I saw you that we'd have loads in common."

Having hoped to create a good impression, a warm glow swept over me. I felt as pleased for Leo as I did for myself. "I'm glad you feel that way."

"Although I never imagined that Jesus would be one of them," Grace said.

My smile vanished. "Excuse me?"

CHAPTER 31

"I can't believe you kept that from me," I said.

With lunch over and the washing up done, Leo and I had decided to get out into the fresh air. Leaving his parents' cottage behind, we made our way down the lane to the beach, with Otis in tow.

"Kept what from you?"

"The fact that you're religious."

Leo looked at me like I'd gone mad. "But I'm not."

I stopped. "Excuse me, you were at that table back there." I indicated the house. "All of us holding hands while your mum thanked the Lord for the food we were about to eat."

Leo chuckled as he continued walking. "You mean when Grace said grace."

"Yes." As his words sank in, I shook my head, refusing to laugh. "It's not funny, Leo. You should have told me."

"Why? Jesus is Mum's thing. Me and Dad just go along with it for her sake."

"So, I knew what to expect. So, I could've been prepared."

"Would it bother you if I was a believer?" Coming to a stop, Leo waited for me to catch up.

"No," I replied, offended that he even had to ask. "But if you can keep something as important as your mum's faith to yourself, I have to wonder what else you're not telling me."

"Rest assured, I have no secrets, religious or otherwise. Although I wouldn't necessarily describe Mum as religious either."

I looked at the man, incredulous. "How can you say that? The woman made us all pray."

Leo smiled. "I meant in any organised sense. Mum's simply… How do I put this? Found the Bible."

"She's a born-again Christian?"

"She's not in the habit of getting a tambourine out, if that's what you mean."

"Come on, you know me better than that."

Picking up pace again, we continued our walk.

"I'm not saying your mum's beliefs bother me. I just think if you had given me the heads-up, she wouldn't now think I'm coming from the same place."

"You're the one who opened the door." Leo chuckled.

"When?" Failing to share his amusement, I couldn't believe he was blaming me.

"What was it Mum said?" He began repeating her words. "*Food for the body and the soul.* And what was your response?" He then repeated mine. "*I can see that.*"

"Which proves my point. I mean, how was I supposed to know she was being literal? If you'd let me in on it, I could have chosen my words more carefully."

"And all the stuff about the Saint Oswald's Church," Leo carried on. "Where did that come from?"

"I was trying to impress."

"You did that all right."

Naturally, I respected Grace's right to her beliefs, even if they were different to mine. What I couldn't understand, was how a simple conversation about a building's history had led her to think I followed Jesus too. "Leo, you should have told me."

As we reached the beachfront, there was no one else in sight. Probably because the locals had more sense, I told myself. I'd never experienced wind like it. Leo unclipped Otis from his lead and the dog ran straight for the water's edge. He barked at the buffeting waves as they crashed onto the sand, and making our way over to him, Leo and I stood in silence staring out at the ocean. Thanks to the grey clouds reflecting on the water, it was hard to see where the horizon ended and the sky began.

"You're right," Leo said, forced to raise his voice to be heard above the roaring sea and the thrashing gale that blew in. "I should have said something."

I pushed my hair out of my face. "Why didn't you?"

"If I'm honest, because I didn't know how. I mean, in what way do you tell someone that your mum likes to quote the Bible? Because believe me, she can be a bit full-on when she wants to." Leo fell quiet for a moment. "Plus, like you said, you'd have steered the conversation differently if you already knew. Been guarded before we'd even arrived." He turned to look at me. "You might not have wanted to meet her at all."

I felt myself relax a little. Put like that, I at least began to understand. We were talking about his mum, after all, and it was only natural that Leo wouldn't want me making false assumptions. However, that didn't stop me from wishing he'd had a bit more faith in me.

Otis appeared with a long piece of driftwood, which he dropped at Leo's feet. Leo picked it up and threw it into the distance and the dog went running after it. "At least now you can see that you're not the only one with an eccentric mother."

"I suppose it explains why you're so patient with my mum. Isn't tolerance one of God's teachings? Your mum obviously passed it on."

Leo scoffed. "Let's just say I've had plenty of practice."

143

"What about Bill?" I recalled his exasperation over their church pilgrimage. "He doesn't seem into it at all. Why doesn't *he* say something?"

"Like I said, we both go along with things out of respect for Mum."

"My dad's the same, I guess. He doesn't stand up for what he does and doesn't want either. Going off their experiences, you have to wonder if opting for the quiet life really is worth it?"

Leo smiled. "I'll let you know when *we* get to that point."

I laughed. "If I turn out to be anything like my mum, I want you to shoot me, not humour me."

"If?" Leo said. His face broke into a smile. "With your dodgy coughs and fake headaches of late, I'd say you're halfway there."

"Cheeky." I took a deep breath of sea air. "Eccentric or not, I'll take your mum's religious stance over mine's wedding obsession any day."

Leo chuckled. "Imagine having both together?"

I shuddered. "I'd rather not."

CHAPTER 32

"*I*'m sorry, son," Bill said. He jumped up from his seat at the table as we let ourselves back into the house. "I tried to stop her."

"What are you talking about?" As we took off our coats and set them to one side with Otis's lead, Leo looked from his dad to me, concerned. He scanned the rest of the room. "Where's Mum?"

"You know what she's like when she gets something into her head. She stops listening to reason."

"Dad, where is she?"

Bill's torso crumpled. "She's on the phone to…"

Before Bill could finish, Grace flew into the room. "I'm so glad you're back," she said, jiggling with excitement. "Because, boy, do I have a surprise for you." She gestured to the dining table. "You're both going to want to sit for this."

Recognising her expression, my stomach sank. Grace had a glint in her eyes; the same kind Mum had when she meddled in our wedding plans.

"What have you done?" Leo asked.

"You, Tess," Grace said. "Will be especially pleased."

I doubted that very much.

Grace's flustering continued. "In fact, I need to sit down myself."

As we all sat, I felt as wary as Leo looked and, while Grace took a moment to compose herself, I took Leo's hand. Coping with my own mum was bad enough, the last thing I needed was Grace's interference too.

"Now, I've just got off the phone to Reverend Joseph."

Leo cocked his head. "Reverend who…?"

As Grace put a hand up to silence her son, I cringed, knowing full well what she was about to tell us.

"At none other than Saint Oswald's church."

"Oh, Lordy," I said, wishing I'd been wrong.

"Oh, Lordy, indeed," Grace replied, with a smile. "And…" She paused, to gather herself for a second time, while I held my breath and willed her not to say it. "He's only agreed to officiate over your wedding."

My grip on Leo's hand tightened.

"He's done what?" Leo asked.

Again, Grace put up her hand to quieten her son. "I know. I was surprised too."

Surprised was not the word running through my head. Nor Leo's and Bill's, going off their faces.

"I'd always assumed you had to be a regular mass goer to get married in church," Grace said. "I only rang on the off-chance. Not that the good news stops there."

"You mean there's more?" Leo said.

I couldn't believe he had to ask. Leo should have known from experience that when it came to mothers and weddings there was always something else.

"Oh, yes. Reverend Joseph has also agreed to oversee your Instruction."

"Our what?" Leo asked.

"And let us consider how we may spur one another toward

love and good deeds," Grace said, with a flourish. "Hebrews, chapter 10, Verses 24-25."

I stared at the woman, dumbfounded.

"It's like a Marriage Preparation course," Grace said. She paused, as if waiting for Leo's reaction. Her eyes narrowed at her son's less than enthusiastic demeanour. "I thought you'd be pleased. After all, courses like this are an opportunity for you to demonstrate your commitment."

Bill shook his head.

"Isn't that what the wedding ceremony's for?" Leo asked.

"Yes, but..." Dismissing her son, Grace turned her attention to me. She smiled. "What do you think, Tess?"

My response took longer than I would have liked, never mind Grace. And while her eyes widened in increased anticipation, I felt my cheeks redden as I tried to come up with the right words. "I think it's kind of you to consider us like this, Grace," I, at last, said. "And Reverend Joseph's offer is certainly something to–"

"That's settled then." Grace slapped her hand on the table, as if to say deal done.

"No, Mum. It's not," Leo said, his tone blunt. "You need to ring back and cancel."

"Why?" Grace stared at him, confused.

"What Leo's trying to say..." Forced to consider what came out of my mouth next, I felt like I was on a verbal tightrope. One wrong word, and things could go horribly amiss which wouldn't bode well for mine and Grace's future relationship. "Is that it's a busy time of year. Workwise, I mean. For both of us. Postponing the marriage preparation course until we've been able to check our diaries makes sense."

Grace didn't appear convinced.

"Isn't that right, Leo?"

He looked at me like I'd gone mad, but I willed him to play along.

"Yes," he said, deadpan. "That makes perfect sense."

I turned back to Grace and gave her a sympathetic smile. "The last thing either of us want is to let Reverend Joseph down," I said. "Arranging something now only to back out later just wouldn't be fair."

Grace let out a despondent sigh. "I suppose when you put it like that. Maybe I should give him another call."

I breathed a sigh of relief.

Another glint appeared in Grace's eyes. "I do have another surprise for you though."

I swallowed hard. "You do?"

Grace put a hand against her chest. "Oh, yes."

Not sure I could take any more, I dreaded to think.

CHAPTER 33

I couldn't believe that Grace had turned out to be as invested in our wedding as much as Mum was. And as Leo and I sat on the edge of the bed staring at the wedding dress hanging on the wardrobe door, it seemed that, yet again, I was the one to pay the price. "It's like I'm being punished," I said.

"I don't know if it's better or worse than the one your mum put forward," Leo said.

With their bedroom directly above ours, we made sure to keep our voices low. The last thing we wanted was for Grace and Bill to hear us.

Unable to take my eyes off it, I took in the dress's every detail. Its sleeves were puffed at the shoulder and tapered to the wrists in a mutton-chop fashion. It had a ruffled, high-neck collar, and a bodice that cinched at the waist. The skirt was a full-on layered tulle affair and while, because of the way the dress hung, I couldn't see the giant bow on the waistline at the back, I knew it was there from when Grace had proudly shown it to me. I let out a sigh. "What am I gonna do?"

"What was it about the eighties and all that rayon fabric?" Leo asked, as mesmerised as I was by the sight in front of us.

"I haven't a clue."

"Why didn't you just say no?" he asked, as if that wasn't a question I'd been asking myself.

"How could I? I'd already said I was having dress issues *and* made excuses over that Marriage Preparation course. Plus, you didn't hear the intense speech she gave, about how she and your dad had never been blessed with a daughter. Apparently, as your life partner, I'm the next best thing. After that, refusing to take it would have been cruel. I couldn't bring myself to do it." A thought suddenly struck me. "Hang on a minute," I said, cocking my head. "I'm not the first to marry into your family. Why didn't Grace offer it to Nial's wife, Victoria?"

"Maybe she did?" Leo said, amused.

"What? And Victoria had the sense to turn it down? Sounds like she'd get on with Sal."

"So, which one are you going to choose? The Princess Diana knock-off?" Leo's voice began to crack. "Or this fetching number?" Unable to control himself any longer, he let out a chuckle. "Better still, you could do a Kardashian and wear both?"

I shook my head. "You're not helping."

CHAPTER 34

The trip to see Bill and Grace hadn't been the carefree break Leo and I had hoped for. However, on the plus side, it had forced us to take ownership of our wedding and while Leo and Otis had gone off to work, I'd spent the morning on the phone, tackling our matrimonial to-do list.

With my head swirling, I was glad when Abbey and Chloe messaged to see if I was up for a video call and unsurprisingly, having seen photos of wedding dress number two, they insisted on a full breakdown as to how it came about.

"This could only happen to you," Abbey said, snorting.

"I haven't laughed this much in ages," Chloe said, clutching her tummy.

I shook my head, with a smile. "Glad to be of service."

"So what are you going to do?" Abbey asked.

"I was hoping you could tell me."

"I can't believe you didn't say thanks but no thanks," Chloe said.

"Believe me, I wish I had."

"Then you'll be pleased to know that we've been talking and have come up with the perfect solution," Abbey said.

"Have we," Chloe said.

"I'm all ears," I said, knowing them far too well to take them seriously.

"A themed wedding," Abbey said, trying but failing to put on a serious face.

"Think about it," Chloe said, giggling. "If *everyone* dresses like an eighties throwback, you won't stand out."

"You could insist on row upon row of shoulder pads."

"And lots of big hair."

"Electric blue mascara."

"And purple eyeshadow and frosted pink lipstick."

The two of them began to properly laugh.

"I can just see you and Leo gliding across the floor to a bit of Spandau Ballet."

"Oh no. The first dance has to be Bill Medley and Jennifer Warnes."

I shook my head again. "You're mad. The pair of you."

"Says the woman who can't turn down a wedding dress when she's offered one. Or should I say two."

"Mummy!" Ruby called out.

Chloe's shoulders slumped. "Just when I was feeling normal instead of sick for a change."

Abbey checked her watch. "I should get off too. The builders will be back from their lunch break soon."

"How're the renovations coming along?" I asked.

"Slower than I'd hoped." Abbey's eyes lit up. "But it's not all doom and gloom."

Chloe and I had seen that twinkle before. It meant she had a man in her sights.

"Mummy!" Ruby wailed again.

Chloe looked crestfallen. "Stop," she said to Abbey and me. "Not another word. No way am I putting this phone down so you two can gossip about gorgeous builders without me."

I laughed. "We wouldn't dream of it."

After promising to chat soon and saying our goodbyes, I continued to smile as I ended the call. My two friends always knew how to cheer me up. However, taking in the numerous notes before me, I supposed I should get back to the task at hand.

I picked up my pen to assess where I'd got to and scanning what I'd written, I was pleased to see I could add at least some blue ticks. We were awaiting emails from a photographer who'd agreed to send samples of her work. We'd sorted our guest list, Leo was organising the flowers, and Sal was making our cake. Mum was overseeing the invites, but those couldn't be sent until we'd decided on where we were getting married, Saint Oswald's church or otherwise.

I frowned as I underlined the word *venue* to signify its importance. No ruling on that left a question mark with regards to our reception and catering. We also had rings to organise, as well as transport for getting to and from the said venue or venues, and Leo needed to sort out his outfit for the day. We still had India as bridesmaid to think about and Sal, as matron of honour. I sighed. Underscoring over and again, the fact that my dress issue had yet to be resolved too.

I put down my pen and feeling at a loss, leaned back in my seat. Having contacted numerous bridal boutiques, everyone I'd spoken to had been sympathetic. But it seemed regardless of my situation, a minimum six-month lead time was needed when it came to having my dream dress made for me or the ones I had altered. Which meant I either had to do a crash course in sewing to create something myself or settle for an off-the-peg number. I chuckled. Or take on board Abbey and Chloe's recommendation that we go for a nineteen-eighties theme.

But that would mean wearing one of the gifted gowns or, as Leo had suggested, both; something I knew I couldn't do even in the name of fun. I scowled, thanks to my cowardliness. Having not yet found the courage to tell Mum and Grace how I felt, I could already picture their upset. Upset that could have been avoided if I'd been open and honest from the off.

"Unless…" An altogether better alternative popped into my head, but just the thought of seeing it through caused my heart rate to increase. I looked down at my notes again, knowing I should at least give it a try. "Come on, Tess," I said, trying to rally myself. "What choice do you have?"

Having exhausted all other avenues, the answer was simple. None.

CHAPTER 35

$\mathcal{B}$y the time I pulled up behind Leo's van, I'd talked myself in and out of my idea numerous times and my doubts continued as I switched off the car engine. Wondering if I should have rung ahead, I looked up at Marianne and Hugo's house hoping to spot Leo so I could get his opinion, but there was no one in sight.

With my hand on the car key and the key still in the ignition, a part of me saw an opportunity to forget the whole thing and turn around again. Another part insisted I had nothing to lose.

Steeling myself, I grabbed my bag and climbed out of the vehicle, before making my way up the path and around to the back of the property. The rear garden was very much the same building site I'd last experienced and while I could hear Leo's voice from somewhere in the distance, craning my neck and glancing around I failed to see him.

Movement through the kitchen window caught my eye and I turned to see Marianne appear at the back door. Just like when we'd previously met, she wore a colourful kaftan, this one made from an exotic parrot print. Her silver hair cascaded down her shoulders, giving her a glamorous yet natural look.

"Tess," she said. "What a lovely surprise." She raised her eyebrows and inclined her head. "That young man of yours hasn't forgotten his lunch again, has he?"

"Not today. So no bacon sandwiches for Hugo, I'm afraid."

"His doctor will be glad to hear it," Marianne said, with a chuckle.

"Actually…" I tried to hide my uncertainty, but it was to no avail. I knew my blushes gave me away. "It's you I came to see."

"Me? That does sound intriguing." She smiled. "Come on in. I'll put the kettle on."

Once inside, Marianne gestured I sit down and while she set about making the drinks, I glanced around the room. Taking in the cheerfulness around me, I rested my hands on the table and toyed with my fingers, determined to summon the courage to explain my situation.

However, dismissing my prior foolishness wasn't that easy and I recalled the ease with which I'd previously chatted with the woman. Having, no doubt, spent years learning her craft, she had to have found my overconfidence insulting.

I took a deep breath, asking myself what was the worst thing that could happen? My eyes settled on the photograph of her and Zane Rafferty. *She could laugh you straight out of the door, that's what.*

Marianne placed a cup in front of me and sat down, before taking a sip from her own. "Now, how can I help?" she asked, with a smile.

"It's about my wedding dress."

Marianne's eyes lit up. "Wonderful. I've been wondering how your sewing's been coming along." She rolled her eyes. "I did ask Leo, but unfortunately I didn't get much of a response."

My cheeks flushed even redder. Admitting that my skill set hadn't lived up to my own hype felt humiliating. But I knew I only had myself to blame. "That's because it's not. I'm rubbish at it."

Marianne's expression softened. She wrinkled her nose. "And you'd like my help?"

I nodded. "More than you know. But I'll understand if you'd rather not. You must have thought me so arrogant the last time I was here. It's just everything's such a mess and…"

"Arrogant?" Marianne seemed surprised I'd say that. "Not at all. I loved your enthusiasm."

"Now you're being kind."

Marianne waved her hand, dismissive. "Tell me. What is it you need?"

Deciding to start at the beginning, I dug my sketchpad out of my bag to show Marianne my dream dress. I took in her smile as she oohed and aahed over the image.

"So simple yet beautiful," she said.

I explained about the number of bedding sheets I'd ruined in my attempts at getting to grips with the sewing machine.

"At least you didn't waste money on fancy fabrics."

And I told her about Mum's Princess Diana heirloom.

Marianne put a hand up to her mouth, but the twinkle in her eyes gave her amusement away. "What a lovely gesture."

Then I explained how I'd managed to inherit Grace's dress too.

"Again, a nice thing to do."

I looked at Marianne direct. "You think?"

Unable to control herself any longer, she sniggered. "No," she said, trying to compose herself. "I think it's a terrible thing to do to someone."

Having outlined everything from start to finish, even I began to see the funny side.

"So what now?" Marianne asked. "And where do I fit in?"

"Obviously I can't wear either of the two dresses I have."

Marianne continued to laugh. "Obviously."

"But at the same time, I don't want to hurt their feelings or let them down." I took a deep breath. "So…"

"You wondered if there was a way of making one new dress, from the two old ones?"

"Yes."

"And I'm guessing as it's wedding season, all the boutiques are busy with their current orders?"

I thought back to the telephone conversations I'd had that morning and nodded.

"Which is why you've come to see me?"

I suddenly felt panicked, realising how awful that looked. "Not that you weren't my first choice. But after insulting your years of experience the way I did, I just wanted to sort the problem out myself."

"Tess, don't worry. You didn't insult me. For all either of us knew, you could have been a natural dressmaker. I mean, some people are." She placed a hand on mine. "Believe me, I'd love to help."

"Really?" After all the gown related stresses and strains, I'd never felt such relief.

"Yes, really." Marianne picked up my sketchpad and assessed the image again. "Now, as lovely as this dress of yours is, why don't we try to come up with something even better?"

Willing myself not to cry, I smiled a grateful smile.

"From what you've described, I think we'll even have enough fabric for a bridesmaid's dress too."

"Oh, I couldn't…"

"And maybe even something for the matron of honour?"

My eyes began to water and wiping them dry, I opened my mouth to tell Marianne that that would be asking too much.

As if reading my mind, she flashed me a silencing look. "See them as a wedding gift. From Hugo and me."

My tears of happiness and relief refused to stop, and lost for words thanks to Marianne's overwhelming kindness, all I could do was nod.

CHAPTER 36

"I can't believe we're doing this," Sal said. "When was the last time we had a fun day out together?"

My sister and I couldn't have been more different. A fun day in my book involved a picnic in the forest, a trip to the seaside, or sitting on my sofa with my feet up reading a good book. It most certainly didn't involve a train ride into the city, to spend hours trawling the shops, hunting for something I could easily have ordered from the comfort of home and have delivered straight to the door. "A while ago," I said. I stared out of the window watching the world go by as we got nearer and nearer to our destination.

"You are allowed to show your excitement, you know. You don't have to keep it to yourself."

My face broke into a smile. "I'm sorry," I said, giving her my full attention. "You know me. I don't have a clue when it comes to fashion and it's not like I ever go anywhere to wear fancy clothes and high heels."

"That's why we're doing this together. You can't get married in a dress made by someone like Marianne only to stick a pair of trainers on your feet. We need to find something in keeping. More exclusive."

I let out a laugh. "Expensive, you mean."

Sal chuckled. "Probably."

"What about you and India? You're both getting new dresses too."

"I know. And I can't tell you how ecstatic I am about it. My very own Zane Rafferty dress."

"Not exactly, Sal."

"It's as good as. Marianne and Zane did work closely together." Sal came over all dreamy. "Who'd have thought it back in the day, eh? When I was pining over the man." She snapped herself back into the present. "Thank you, Tess. It's because of your struggles that I'm getting this dress and I won't forget it. As for our shoes, me and India can sort ourselves out another time. Today is about you."

The train began to slow as it approached Leeds City station. Coming to a stop, Sal and I rose to our feet and, along with our fellow passengers, disembarked. While we walked at a normal pace, everyone around us seemed to race toward the exit. Watching them dodge and weave around each other to get there first, I was reminded why I didn't go to the city very often. I much preferred the calm of the countryside to the metropolitan bustle. Unlike Sal, I noted, who was buzzing.

"I hope you've brought your credit card," she said. "Retail therapy, here we come."

Whereas I'd have been more than happy to source my wedding shoes online, for a shopaholic like my sister, Leeds wasn't just *the* place to go, it was paradise. After dragging me from store to store, I didn't doubt that by the end of the day I'd be as spent as my savings.

A business-type chap bumped into my shoulder as he hurried past.

My sister frowned. "Excuse me!" Sal called after him when no apology was forthcoming.

"Sal," I said, embarrassed by her outburst.

"What? Someone's got to stick up for you because you don't stick up for yourself." She shook her head, glaring at the chap as he disappeared into the crowd. "Some people."

Jostling our way off the platform, we stepped out onto the street. I looked around, confused, with no idea as to the direction we should take.

Sal grinned. "Don't worry," she said, linking her arm through mine. "I know exactly which way to go."

Guiding me along one thoroughfare after another, we arrived at Victoria Quarter, an arcade full of theatrical grandeur in the heart of the city's shopping area. A spectacular Grade-II listed landmark, it was designed by Frank Matcham back in 1900, the very same architect who designed the London Palladium. It wasn't a place I visited often, but I knew exactly what to expect.

"Sal, this is so not me," I said. Home to the likes of Louis Vuitton, Mulberry, Reiss and a huge five-floor Harvey Nichols, the place couldn't have been more out of my comfort zone.

Sal smiled. "After you," she said, completely ignoring my complaint.

As I did as I was told, I couldn't deny the place's magnificence and I immediately admired its marble columns, pink terracotta facades, gilt mosaics and wrought-iron detail. Awed by the splendour, my gaze moved upwards to the stained-glass roof that sat above stunning intricate murals. "You wouldn't think this area used to be all slaughterhouses and slums," I said, turning my attention to the lines of traditional rich-mahogany shopfronts.

"Yeah, yeah, yeah," Sal said. "Now come on."

Pulling me along with her, our search for the perfect shoes began in earnest. But while my sister swooned at display after display, my heart sank further and further. No matter the shop, label or cost, I simply couldn't find anything I liked. Everything was too high, or too fancy, and when I did try a pair on, too uncomfortable.

"Shoe shopping should not be this hard," Sal said, as we exited yet another store.

"Time for a break?" I asked, hopeful. "A cup of coffee, maybe?"

Sal looked at me like I'd lost the plot. "Not until we've got what we came for. I will not be beaten by sodding footwear." She looked up and down the arcade as if deciding her next move. "By my reckoning, we only have one shop left to try, and I don't think you're going to like it."

"Why not? Which shop?"

"Sorry, Tess, but you're going to have to trust me on this. Come on."

My shoulders slumped at the thought of taking another step. I felt like I'd walked miles already and my feet certainly weren't up for squeezing into yet another pair of stilettos.

"There's no point sulking," Sal called back. "Like I've already said, you're not walking down the aisle in anything less than your dress deserves."

Grumbling to myself, I traipsed behind. "Yes, Mum."

"I heard that," Sal replied, still refusing to abort her mission.

Finally, we came to a standstill.

I took in the shop's signage. "You're kidding me?" I said. If the other stores didn't have anything suitable, no way would the one before us hold the answer.

"At least have a look inside before you make judgement."

I stared through the window and taking in the brightly coloured pencil mini dress that hung on display, I tried to figure out if its pattern was world flag or Picasso inspired. Even more confusing, was the long fitted maxi dress on offer. Dark metallic grey in finish, it was long sleeved, and had two weird overlapping front panels that created a draping effect. The high thigh split detail was eye-watering, and as edgy and forward thinking as the dress no doubt was, I couldn't for a second think where such an ensemble could be worn. "Sal, this is Vivienne Westwood. Famous for punk rock and tartan." I glanced down at my fitted white T-shirt and straight-legged cropped jeans. "Do I even remotely fall into this shop's demographic?"

"There's a first time for everything," Sal said, taking my arm and shoving me through the door.

A member of staff looked up from the counter as we entered. She was around my age, but that's where the similarity between us ended. She wore a long-length bright red shirt under a navy and white checked suit, and a thick large-silver-buckled belt around her waist. Her hair was long, poker straight, and black, and her fringe was cut into a widow's peak. Her make-up was faultless. Winged eyeliner swept across her lids, creating the perfect hood effect and her bright red lipstick had been meticulously applied.

"I don't know why we're even bothering," I said. Keeping my voice low, I was convinced that the shop assistant had to be thinking the same thing.

"Excuse me," Sal said, marching straight up to the woman.

"Yes," she replied. "How can I help?"

"Shoes," Sal said. "My sister here is getting married soon, and we've looked everywhere for the right pair. You're our last hope."

The woman turned to me and going from my head to my toes, her eyes settled on my comfortable runners. She diverted her attention back to Sal, screwing up her face as she spoke. "I'm not sure we're the right place for–"

Sal raised her eyebrows, warning the woman not to finish her sentence. "I take it you've heard of Zane Rafferty?"

"Sal!" I couldn't believe she was pulling the name card.

"Who hasn't?" the shop assistant said. "A great designer. And well ahead of his time."

"Exactly. And a member of his team just happens to be the head designer of Tessa here's wedding dress. Suffice to say, the designer concerned shall remain nameless. But we both know that since Mr Rafferty's death, one or two of his underlings have gone on to earn worldwide fame themselves."

The shop assistant fixed a smile on her face. "Would you like to come this way?"

CHAPTER 37

*H*aving shoe shopped until we dropped, my sister and I needed sustenance and in the mood for a casual dining experience as opposed to fancy and formal, we headed to a little street café Sal knew. Apparently they had a selection of fabulously tasty cakes and all of them home-made, which was high praise indeed from my cake-maker extraordinaire sister.

"Here we are," she said, pointing just ahead.

I smiled at the sight. Thanks to my aching feet, never had a seating area felt so welcoming. Wicker chairs and bistro tables were lined up in a Parisian fashion and a retractable all-weather canopy had been wound out to protect customers from the sun. Abundant flower installations containing white and pink roses sat at either end. It was the perfect spot to sit and watch the world go by.

"You grab a couple of seats," Sal said. "I'll get the coffee."

Knowing I couldn't stand in line even if I wanted to, I wasn't about to argue. "Don't forget the cake," I said, calling after her.

Sal chuckled. "I won't."

I spotted a free table in the middle of the row and heading straight for it, I plonked myself and my bags down. With the chair taking my weight, my burning feet had never felt so appreciative. I smiled at the young couple sat next to me. If they hadn't been eating, I'd have taken off my runners and given my toes and heels a much-needed rub.

"Here you go," Sal said, reappearing with a tray of goodies. She lifted off a latte and placed it in front of me. "Will this do you?" She passed me a side plate on which sat a huge piece of red velvet sponge.

"You're an angel," I said. Just looking at it, I could taste the hint of cocoa and cream cheese frosting and as Sal set her own drink down and put the tray to one side, I picked up my fork and dived straight in. I closed my eyes. "Heavenly," I said, as soon as the smooth, soft texture hit my tongue.

"Can I?" Sal said, indicating my Vivienne Westwood paper carrier bag.

"If you must."

Sal giggled as she picked it up. Pulling out the shoebox, she stroked and admired it, before lifting off the lid to reveal the delights within. "They're simply beautiful," she said. "Classic and modern at the same time." She took a deep breath and slowly exhaled. "I'm so jealous of you right now, you wouldn't believe."

According to the shop assistant, the blush pink shoes were made in Italy from recycled satin. They were a peep-toe design and had a gold buckle on the strap that fastened around the ankle. Finished with a leather outer sole and heel, the shoe's fabric had been laser cut to create slashed detailing. They were a far cry from any footwear I was used to.

Sal popped the lid back on and secreted the box back into the bag. "Once the wedding's over," she said, as she handed everything back, "you'd better keep wearing them. Shoes like that should be shown off. Not dumped at the bottom of the wardrobe never to be seen again."

I laughed. "At that price, I'll definitely be getting my money's worth. I'll never have them off."

"Tess!" a woman's voice rang out.

Glancing over Sal's shoulder, I spotted a woman waving my way as she dashed towards us. Frowning, I wondered who she was.

"I thought it was you." The woman looked from me to my sister. "And Sal too. How lovely to see you both."

The woman, who I put in her forties, wore a crisp white shirt and grey linen trousers. A red barrel handbag hung off her forearm and her hair was short in a pixie-cut style. Taking in her smile, I sort of recognised her, but as my mind raced, I couldn't place where from.

"It's me. Cousin Annie," she said. "I'm not surprised you didn't realise." She put a hand up to her hair. "I'm trying out a new look."

"Oh, yes," Sal said, her face lighting up. "Annie."

The name did not mean anything to me.

"So how have you been?" my sister asked.

"Good, thanks. Busy with the children, of course." Her expression turned proud. "And Derek finally got his promotion."

"That's wonderful to hear," Sal said, while I wondered who the hell Derek was.

Annie directed her attention back to me. "And I believe you're soon to be married?"

I shifted in my seat and while I smiled on the outside, on the inside I wondered how the woman, who, to all intents and purposes, was a stranger, would know that.

"Your mum was telling me all about it," Annie said.

I pursed my lips. Of course she was. Having told anyone and everyone, by all means available, why wouldn't Mum break the news to a cousin I couldn't even remember.

"She's ever so excited about it," Annie said.

"She certainly is," I replied.

"Not long to go now though, eh?" Annie sighed. "A September wedding. The perfect time of year, don't you think?"

SUZIE TULLETT

"One of the reasons we chose it," I said, keeping my tone light.

"Not too hot, not too cold," Sal said.

Eyes wide, Annie looked at me direct. "I can't wait to receive my invite."

Her tone went up at the end and I wasn't sure if she'd asked me a question or assumed there was an invitation in the post.

"Anyway, things to do, people to see," Annie said, gesturing it was time for her to leave.

"Well, it's been lovely catching up, Annie," Sal said. "And please, pass on my congratulations to Derek."

"Oh, I will. Thank you."

Watching the woman head off, I waited until she was out of earshot before speaking. "You don't know who she is, do you?"

Sal shook her head. "Haven't a clue."

CHAPTER 38

"Yes, Mum. We'll be there." With my phone to my ear, I perched on the edge of the sofa, desperate to end the call. I had a lot to do and the last thing I wanted was to waste time chatting, especially when we were all seeing each other the following day.

"Good," she said. "Because I've got some great news for you both about the wedding."

My back stiffened. "Really?" I pictured her excitement.

"Don't worry. You'll love it."

While I doubted that very much, the line fell silent, as if Mum was waiting for me to press further for details.

"Oh, Tess, I can't wait to see the smile on your face," she said, when I did nothing of the sort.

I considered my mother's prior matrimonial endeavours, all the while dreading what her *news* might be. I knew from experience it wasn't going to be good, and as much as I wanted to give in and push her on the matter, I decided against it. The next few hours called for a delicate hand, not jittery fingers resulting from more upset. "Whatever it is, we can talk about it tomorrow," I said. "Anyway, I've got to go."

"But…"

"Bye, Mum." I put the phone down. Taking a deep breath, I gathered myself before getting up to join Leo in the kitchen.

"Everything okay?" he said, as I trundled into the room.

"Yes and no." Heading for the coffee machine, I poured us both a cup. Taking a sip of mine, I leant against the countertop. "I've just got off the phone to Mum." I attempted a smile.

"Go on."

"Apparently she has news."

Putting his cup to his lips, he looked at me, quizzical.

"About the wedding."

"Ah." Leo chuckled. "Does that mean we have another phantom headache to look forward to?" he said, clearly recalling the morning of our last Cavendish get-together.

"Funny," I said, pulling a face. "And before you ask, I haven't a clue what the news is. I'll let her tell us face to face."

"Delaying the inevitable, eh?"

"Oh, yes. Plus, we have more important things to think about." I checked the time. "Like the fact that Sal, Ryan, and India will be landing shortly."

"Since when?"

"Since about ten minutes ago. I rang them before talking to Mum."

Leo stared at me, bemused.

"You've seen all the fabric that needs unpicking," I said.

Leo frowned. "So this means…?"

"It's a group activity? Oh, yes. It's all hands on deck until it's done, even if that means working 'til midnight." I downed the last of my drink. "I still don't know how I'm going to break what I'm doing to Mum. Or Grace. They love those dresses."

Leo's mobile rang. He picked it up and checked the screen. "Speaking of whom."

I scoffed. "Maybe your mum has news too?"

Leo shook his head. "Don't even joke about it." Declining the call, he placed his phone down on the side and gave me his full attention. "So, did Patricia have anything else to say?"

"Only that Dad's off to some golfing tournament."

Leo smiled. "A golfing tournament, you say?"

"I don't know what's so funny. I think it's great he's got a new interest. Anyway, enough about my parents. Let's talk wedding plans. Did you look at those samples the photographer sent through?"

"I did."

"And?"

"I think they're great. I'm happy to go with her if you are?"

"Brilliant." I headed to the table where my to-do list sat. "Can you email her back and book her in?"

"I can."

Picking up my pen, I put a big blue tick next to the photographer's name. "Obviously we can't give her any location details yet." I looked to Leo again. "We still haven't discussed whether we're happy to go with your mum's religious ceremony or stick with our original plan and take the civil route." I pictured the church's interior with its wooden pews and stone arches. I saw rainbows of colour as sunlight entered through its stained-glass windows and heard the bell ring out from its tower. "Maybe we shouldn't cancel Reverend Joseph and Saint Oswald's quite yet?"

"I'm okay with that if you are," Leo replied.

"It's not like we have an alternative, is it?" I smiled. "Who'd have thought that way back when there was a chance I'd get married in the same church I was learning about."

"All the more reason not to dismiss it."

"It would certainly keep your mum happy. The last thing I want is her thinking bad of us. Or more to the point, of me. Especially when we've only just met." I scanned my list again, happy that things were coming together at last. "You know, I can't thank Marianne enough. It's because of her kindness that

SUZIE TULLETT

I've stopped worrying about dresses and can properly concentrate on all this. I'm determined to make sure that from now on there'll be no unnecessary complication. Just me and you and no one else. Getting on with it. Once the unstitching's done, of course."

"Which reminds me," Leo said. His mobile rang, but again he declined the call. "You're not the only one to move forward on something." He headed out into the hallway, before returning with a sketchpad. "What do you think of this?"

I smiled. "Is this my bouquet?"

Leo nodded.

My heart melted as I took in the arrangement. Full of blue, purple, and yellow flowers, it was made up of daisy-like fleabane, nodding devil's-bit, delicate eyebright, and snapdragon-esque toadflax. Its foliage was a mix of grass and sedge, with natural twine keeping the whole ensemble in position. I looked from the drawing to my husband-to-be. "It's beautiful. Perfect."

Leo looked back at me. His stare intense, he leaned down to kiss me.

Butterflies fluttered in my tummy, and I closed my eyes, anticipating the feel of his lips on mine. His mobile rang again, and my eyes flashed open.

"She's not going to give up, is she?" Leo said of his mum.

I shook my head.

"Mum," he said, as he reluctantly took the call. "Lovely to hear from you." Leo's eyes narrowed as Grace began to talk. "But..." He frowned my way. "I see." His mother talked some more. "I guess that makes sense."

Taking in his seriousness, I willed him to tell me what was going on. But Grace's continued chatter meant rather than relay back to me, Leo had to listen. And the more he listened, the more disheartened he appeared, while I sat hoping things weren't as bad as his expression seemed to indicate.

172

"When?" Leo said. "Okay… Yeah… You too." At last, the call came to an end.

"What was that about?" I asked.

He took a deep breath as he tucked his phone in his pocket. "You know how you said you were looking forward to us having time to focus on the wedding?"

"Yes."

"Me, you, and no one else?"

"Yes."

"With no unnecessary complications."

"Please just tell me."

"They've decided to come over. Mum and Dad. For a visit."

"But why? It's not like we haven't seen them recently."

"Mum thinks it would be a good idea for everyone to meet before the wedding."

My heart sank. "When you say everyone?"

"Us, them, the rest of your family."

"You're kidding me?"

"They're researching flights as we speak. Apparently they want to prevent any social awkwardness on the big day."

"I see." Cringing at the prospect, I wasn't sure I was ready for such an introduction. "Don't get me wrong, I understand where Grace and Bill are coming from…"

"But?" Leo said.

I stared at Leo. Having known my family for as long as he had, I couldn't believe he had to ask.

CHAPTER 39

*H*aving pushed the family introduction issue to the back of my mind, I couldn't help but smile at the sight of my workforce. Leo, Sal, Ryan, and India were working diligently to help me deconstruct the two wedding dresses. Grateful for their assistance, I knew I couldn't have managed on my own.

My attention went from them to the mess surrounding us. The lounge looked like an explosion in a bridal factory. Every surface was covered in either charmeuse, organza, chiffon, tulle, or lace. I couldn't see him, but I knew even Otis was amongst the chaos somewhere.

I placed an individual bodice panel from Grace's dress on my lap and smoothed it out. "Goodbye, nineteen-eighties," I said. "Hello, twenty-first century."

"I'm surprised at how therapeutic this is," Sal said. Seam rippers in hand, she and Ryan tackled a skirt section of Mum's wedding gown.

"You think?" Ryan replied, frowning.

"It's all in a good cause," I said, before turning my attention to Leo. "You okay there?"

Working with a pained expression, he appeared to be struggling.

"It's all right for you lot with your nimble fingers," he said, reaching for a pair of scissors. "But when you've got gardener's hands like mine." He snipped at a strand of cotton, before suddenly downing tools. "You know what? I need a break." He glanced around. "Anyone hungry?"

I smiled. Leo's offer of sustenance came as no surprise. More adept with a spatula and a frying pan than any sewing paraphernalia, Leo's primary contribution was always going to be keeping the rest of us fed and watered. In fact, I was surprised he'd sat there for as long as he had. "Starving," I said, giving him the out he wanted.

"Then why don't I rustle something up?"

"I'll help," Ryan said. Seizing the opportunity, he rose to his feet and stretched himself out. "If nothing else, it might restore my eyesight."

"India, how are you doing?" I asked, as the two men disappeared off into the kitchen. "Do you need a break too?"

"I'm fine," she replied. Keeping her focus, she pushed her hair from her face. "It's good to have a hand in what I'll be wearing for my first walk."

"You mean when you're the bridesmaid and *I'm* the maid of honour?" Sal said.

India paused to look at me. "Do you think Marianne–"

Sal giggled at the name. Having been Zane Rafferty's number one fan, the prospect of having her very own dress made by one his closest employees obviously tickled her. And while India shook her head at her mum, no doubt for being childish, I imagined the pair in their brand-new dresses, striding, hands on hip, up the aisle. One for career reasons, one out of pride.

"As I was saying," India said, causing her mother to laugh some more. "Do you think she'll introduce me to her contacts?"

I smiled. While I often found India a tad overconfident, I

couldn't deny her ambition. Be her a scientist, a professional mourner, or a fashion model, the girl went for it. Hence her attire. Blue shorts, a red T-shirt and a bright yellow cardigan, India had obviously taken inspiration from Marianne and Zane Rafferty. Add to that a string of chunky green wooden beads and an array of colourful bangles on her wrist, India wanted to impress.

"Although I can't see why she wouldn't," India said, in answer to her own question. "I mean look at me." She swept her hair to one side again, as we all got back to unpicking the dresses.

"What's this?" The first to break the silence, Sal frowned and pulling whatever it was free, held it up.

"A dry-cleaning label," I said, recalling how it had scratched my thigh when Mum first insisted I try the dress on.

Sal gave it a closer look. "It's not, you know." Bemused, she turned her attention to me. "It's a price tag." She shifted forward in her seat and held it out for me to take. "Here. Check it out."

I squinted as I tried to make out the faded writing. "You're right," I said, surprised by what I was looking at. "It's even got the name of the boutique on it." I looked to my sister, confused. "But why was it still attached?"

"Mum must have forgotten to take it off," Sal said.

"Well, there's no other explanation," I said.

India stopped what she was doing and looked at us both like we were stupid. "Are you two for real?"

"Excuse me?" I said.

"It's there because Grandma and Grandad aren't married," India said.

Sal laughed. "Of course they are. What on earth gave you that idea?"

"More to the point, why would Mum give me someone else's wedding dress?"

India continued to stare at us like we were lacking. "Have you ever seen evidence of this alleged union?"

I thought for a moment and forced to concede that I hadn't, I looked to Sal who shrugged, enough to tell me that she hadn't either.

"And don't you think, knowing what Grandma is like, there'd be at least one great big photo of the event hanging where everyone could see it?"

I had to question if the girl had a point. Huge pictures aside, not only hadn't I seen a wedding album, I couldn't recall even a framed snapshot of Mum and Dad's big day. I looked to my sister again. "Nah," I said, dismissing the idea. "We'd know if they weren't."

"Of course we would," Sal said.

Sal and I gave it a second before we both jumped out of our seats and raced to the kitchen to get Leo and Ryan's take on the matter.

"Great timing," Leo said, as he placed a plate of sandwiches on the table.

"Leo was just telling me his parents are coming over," Ryan said. "Apparently they want to meet us all before the wedding."

"As much as I can't wait to meet them," Sal said, dismissive. "What do you think of this?" She handed the tag to Ryan.

"It's a pricing label," he said, clearly wondering what the fuss was about.

"Exactly!"

Ryan looked back at her, bemused.

"Off Mum's wedding dress," Sal said.

"So?" Ryan said. "Maybe she forgot to take it off."

"India doesn't think Mum and Dad are married," I said.

"India? How would she know?" Ryan scoffed. "You two weren't even born back then, never mind her."

Sal and I shared a look, realising he had a point.

"And something like that would be pretty hard to keep quiet over the years," I said, accepting Ryan's reasoning.

"You're right," Sal said. "India's claim doesn't make sense. Of course Mum and Dad are married."

Leo grabbed knives and forks from the cutlery drawer. "Would it be a problem if they weren't?"

"Not really," Sal said.

"Of course not," I said.

"Well then?"

"But it's not as simple as that, is it?" I replied. "If our parents aren't married, why would Mum insist on passing down a dress that isn't even hers? Why call it an heirloom?"

"I bet you ten pounds they're not," India said, entering the room.

Sal suddenly screamed, horrified at the sight of her daughter. "What have you *done?*"

As Ryan, Leo and I spun round, all thoughts of Mum and Dad disappeared into the ether. We each stood wide-eyed and in shock, taking in the pair of scissors India held in one hand, and the long clump of hair she held in the other.

India's gaze went from her mum to her dad, to Leo, and then to me. "What? It was getting in my eyes. It needed a trim," she said. "Plus, if I'm going to make it as a supermodel, I need to be edgy. How else am I going to stand out?"

"But you've..." Sal let out a whimper.

I stared at what I assumed was supposed to be India's new fringe. Sitting a couple of inches above her eyebrows and about a centimetre below her hairline, it appeared India had trimmed to the extreme. With only a couple of months to the wedding, another picture of her following me down the aisle popped into my head. "How quickly does her hair grow, Sal?"

CHAPTER 40

"Something smells good," Leo said.

Hanging our jackets on the banister, he and I had just landed at Mum and Dad's. After the excitement of dropping off sack loads of fabric at Marianne's house, we'd spent the rest of our car journey trying to guess what wedding news Mum could possibly have. Leo gave me a wink. No doubt, another of his attempts to reassure me all would be well. I only hoped he was right; that the day wasn't about to take a turn for the worst.

Mum smiled, appreciating the compliment. "Slow-cooked pork shoulder, crispy roast potatoes, pork and herb stuffing, with caramel glazed parsnips and carrots."

"Very nice," Leo said.

"All served on the finest of bone china."

Mum's dinner service had been her pride and joy since I could remember. "We wouldn't expect anything else," I said.

"And for dessert?" Leo asked.

"Dark fruit crumble with vanilla custard." She gestured to the lounge. "Now, you two go through, while I check how things are going in the kitchen."

Having expected Mum to share what she had to say at the first opportunity, I watched her head off down the hall.

Leo leaned into me. "Didn't I tell you it wouldn't be that big of a deal?"

We entered the lounge to the sight of Dad giggling over some video on his phone.

"What's that you're watching?" I asked. Curious as to who the excitable voice emanating from the screen belonged to, I approached to find out. However, Dad quickly hit the stop button and shut down the video.

"Nothing," he said, sliding the mobile into his shirt's chest pocket.

I eyed him suspiciously, but before I could question him further, Mum breezed into the room. Clasping her hands together, she positioned herself in front of everyone, and wearing a big smile, stared at Leo and me. "Now."

I flashed Leo a look. Recognising Mum's expression, it seemed the moment had come.

Dad jumped up from his seat. "Drink, anyone?" He evidently knew what Mum was about to reveal, and his speediness did nothing for my confidence.

"Wine if you've got it, please," I said, tempted to ask for the bottle.

"It's only us!" Sal called out from the hallway.

Mum's glee intensified. "Ooh, goody. Now we can all revel in the excitement."

My sister, Ryan, and India trudged into the lounge.

"Oh. My. Word." Mum's jaw dropped and her joy turned to horror at the sight of her granddaughter.

"What?" India asked, as if semi-scalping herself was nothing.

"I'm sorry, Tess," Sal said. "We've tried everything to hide it." She lifted the sides of her daughter's hair and swept it first one way and then the other in a comb-over fashion. But no matter Sal's attempts, India's locks kept springing back. "Nothing I do seems to work." Turning her attention back to me, Sal sighed. "Honestly, I can't apologise enough."

"Believe me, her days as a fashion model are well and truly over," Ryan said, his tone stern.

"We understand if you've changed your mind about her being bridesmaid," Sal said.

India rolled her eyes at all the fuss.

Mum scoffed. "Of course, she can't walk–"

"We haven't changed our minds," Leo said. Interrupting my mother before she could finish, he smiled at India.

Mum let out a whimper.

"Have we, Tess?"

"That's assuming *you* still want the role, India?" I asked. A part of me hoped that she'd say no. Not being photogenic myself, the wedding pictures were going to be bad enough without her assistance. However, another part hoped that she'd say yes, because at least then I wouldn't be alone in ruining them.

India shrugged. "Why wouldn't I? It's only hair."

Observing India's innocence, I suddenly felt humbled. It seemed Leo had been right to suggest I was more like my mother than I cared to admit. More concerned about the quality of our wedding album than the true value of our day, I'd clearly lost sight of what mattered – being surrounded by the people we love. I smiled at India. "I agree."

Dad reappeared with a tray of glasses and while he shook his head and chuckled at his granddaughter's hair, Mum grabbed one, put it straight to her mouth, and drained it of its contents.

"What is it with this family?" she asked.

"Speaking of families," Leo said. "Mum and Dad are coming over and would like to meet you all."

"Really?" Mum replied, perking up again. "How lovely."

"They're hoping to prevent any awkwardness at the wedding. You know, Tess's family on one side, mine on the other, no one daring to mix."

"What a great idea," Dad said. He trained his eyes on Mum. "At least someone's thinking straight."

Ignoring Dad's quip, Mum's eyes widened. "Oh, yes. My news." She nodded to Dad, indicating he should hand the rest of us a drink, and taking a deep breath, she looked to Leo and me. "You know how you visited Gregbrook Manor as a potential wedding venue?"

Ryan leaned into Sal, but before he could speak she shushed him.

"Yes," I replied, cautious.

"And that you said it wasn't suitable?"

"It wasn't. It was too big," Leo said.

Dad proffered us the tray and encouraging us to take a glass, we did as we were told.

"Well…" Mum's smile got bigger. "You'll be pleased to know that's no longer a concern."

I narrowed my eyes. "What do you mean?" I asked.

"It means I've booked it." She clapped her hands together. "That's where you're getting married."

Recalling all the other lines Mum had crossed, my back stiffened. "You've done what?"

As I took a deep breath, scared I'd say something I'd only regret, Sal nudged Ryan and gestured he take India out of the way.

"Why do I have to miss out on the action?" he asked, his voice low. My sister glowered and realising he had no choice, Ryan sighed. "Come on, India. Let's go and see how dinner's coming along."

"I've arranged for Gregbrook Manor to do the wedding," Mum said, in answer to my question.

"But why would you do that?" I asked. "Like Leo just pointed out, it's too big. And not only–"

"Correction," Mum said. "It *was* too big."

"Excuse me?" Watching Mum head out of the room, I felt Leo take my hand.

"I'm sorry, love," Dad said, while I continued to fume. "By the time I realised what she was up to, it was too late."

Mum reappeared with a stack of wedding invitations. It consisted of way more than the twenty-odd that Leo and I had asked her to sort out.

"Please tell me you haven't?" I said.

"It all started when I saw cousin Annie."

Sal and I glanced at each other, realising she meant the woman we'd spoken to on our shoe shopping trip.

Mum turned to Dad. "When we were at the supermarket that day. You remember?"

Dad threw his hands up. "Don't bring me into this."

"Anyway, you two were in Ireland," Mum said, turning back to Leo and me. "And I was telling her about the wedding and how, through not having a venue, I couldn't send out the invitations. Which is when she said that explained why she hadn't yet received hers. Of course, I couldn't tell her she wasn't getting one."

"Why not?" I asked.

Mum looked at me like I'd gone mad. "Because that would have been embarrassing. Anyway, that's when it hit me. If I made the wedding party bigger, both our problems would be sorted. You'd get a venue that you love…"

I scoffed. "And you don't have to tell cousin Annie that she can't come to the wedding."

"Exactly." Mum tilted her head and wrinkled her nose. "I knew you'd understand."

I forced myself to breathe.

"Naturally, this lot only pertains to the Cavendishes." Mum indicated the invitation stack. "So, to even things out, I'll need names and addresses of any extra guests on your side, Leo."

Unable to listen to anymore, I rose to my feet. "I'm going home."

"What do you mean?" Mum looked at me, bewildered. "We haven't had dinner yet." She took a step towards me.

"Mother," Sal said. She shook her head, as if warning Mum to leave it.

"But I thought they'd be happy." Mum looked to me and Leo.

"Did you really though?" I asked, my frustration getting the better of me. "I mean, from day one you've wanted some big fancy wedding." I felt my pulse race; the result of mine and Leo's stupidity, as much as it was Mum's actions. I gestured to her pile of envelopes. "Of course, it's our own fault. For putting you in charge of invitations in the first place. Let's face it, after the mood boards and that bloody dress, we should have seen it coming."

"What's wrong with my dress?" Mum asked. "And why's Gregbrook Manor suddenly a problem? If you're worried about money, Tess, your dad and I have covered it."

I glared at Mum. I didn't think I'd ever felt so insulted. "Have you listened to a single word I've said these last weeks? This has got nothing to do with…" Falling silent, I shook my head. "You know what. I give up."

"I don't understand," Mum said.

"Then shame on you, Mum," I replied. Desperate to keep my anger in check, I turned to Leo. "We need to leave."

Leo appeared hesitant.

"Now."

CHAPTER 41

The silence on the drive home was deafening. I wanted to speak, but every time I tried, I couldn't find the right words to express the myriad angry thoughts running through my mind. Leo's instinct clearly told him to give me headspace, something I appreciated and turning to him for the umpteenth time, I opened my mouth to tell him that, only to close it again.

"It'll be okay," Leo said, when we, at last, pulled up.

"Will it? Because I'm not so sure."

After climbing out of the car, Leo unlocked the cottage front door to let us in.

Having left Otis at home snoozing after his long morning walk, we entered to find him wagging his tail at our arrival. I gave him a cursory fuss, before heading straight down the hall to the kitchen. I tossed my bag on the table and slumped down on a chair. "What was she thinking?"

"I'm sure she meant well," Leo said. Coming up behind me, he wrapped his arms around my shoulders, but I shrugged myself free. I twisted in my seat to face him.

"The last thing I need right now is you defending her. What Mum's done is unforgivable. Why can't you see that?"

"I understand what you're saying, but–"

"There are no buts, Leo. The whole thing's ruined. The wedding that we talked about, that I thought we both wanted, has gone forever." He stepped towards me. However, reassurance was the last thing I needed. I wanted him to tell me that he was as frustrated as I was, not that Mum's heart was in the right place. "It's *our* day, Leo. Not hers." I waited for him to tell me he was on my side.

"I know that." He put one hand on his hip, while running the other through his hair. "I also think she can't help herself. Excitement takes over and she genuinely thinks she's helping."

I wanted to scream at Leo. Ask him why he had to be so nice about everyone and everything all the time. However, I knew that wouldn't be fair. Leo might defend Mum, but he wasn't to blame for everything that had happened. She was. "So that's it? That's all you've got to say on the matter?"

Leo stood there silent.

"And what about the knock-on effect? Like all the extra flower arrangements that we're going to have to sort out. The extra photos. Extra everything when you think about it. You do realise September isn't that far off, don't you?"

"We'll sort it." Just like Mum, Leo didn't seem to get it.

Realising I was talking to myself, I decided I was done with arguing. I shook my head, defeated. In need of some space, I headed for the back door. "If you want me, I'll be in my workshop."

CHAPTER 42

$\mathcal{I}$n no mood to create, I'd spent goodness knew how long organising the implements of my trade. I was surprised at how many pieces of equipment I'd accumulated over the years and methodically sorting through my various hand tools had helped ease my furious mind. A tap at the door interrupted me and expecting to see Leo pop his head round, I was surprised to find Sal making an appearance instead.

"Fancy a break?" she asked, indicating the mugs of tea she'd brought with her.

I smiled, pleased to see her.

Sal nodded to the wooden bench just outside. "Out here in the sunshine?"

Stepping into the fresh air, I sat down next to her. I closed my eyes for a moment and breathed in the scent of the garden.

"How are you feeling?"

"Annoyed, frustrated, resentful."

"Mum says she's sorry, if that's any consolation." Sal handed me my drink.

I sneered. "Sorry I'm not grateful?"

My sister chuckled. "For the upset she's caused."

"Bet she still doesn't know why I feel the way I do though, eh?"

Sal shook her head. "Not really, no. But she did try to understand."

"I suppose that's something." I sighed. "Why does she do these things, Sal?"

"I'm not going to even try to figure out how that woman's brain works."

I sipped on my tea. "Leo thinks she's trying to help."

"For what it's worth, so do I."

I looked at Sal, aghast. "Really?"

"As much as she's a pain in the ass and I'm convinced would like nothing more than to compete with the likes of Louise Patterson, she isn't vindictive. There's more to it. She genuinely thinks she's being supportive and making sure you have the best of everything. And once she gets an idea in her head…"

"There's no stopping her?"

"Exactly."

"To be fair, she said as much herself. After introducing me to her wedding planner friend." As I pictured Gregbrook Manor's beautiful orangery, packed with people I barely knew, I wondered what it was about small and intimate that Mum didn't get? "It's just not the wedding we want, Sal. And now she's paid out a fortune, how can we say no? Even if she only handed over a deposit, it'll be a sum and a half, and I bet it's non-refundable."

"Simply thank her for the offer and tell her it's not for you."

"Is that what you'd do?"

"If I could afford to pay her outlay back, then yes."

"And if you couldn't?"

Sal fell quiet for a moment. "On another note, it was good to see you stick up for yourself for once."

"It didn't feel good. Why do you think I walked out?"

My sister smiled. "Between the two of us, you've always been the lover. I'm the fighter."

I pondered over our differences. "Why is that? Why do you get to be stubborn and defiant, while I'm anything but?"

"Because I'm the oldest, maybe?"

"I hope you're not suggesting I've been babied. We share the same mother, remember."

Sal laughed. "You definitely take after Dad."

"Does that mean you take after…?"

"Don't even say it."

With my thoughts returning to the matter at hand, I took a deep breath and exhaled. "Well, it looks like our little church ceremony is off."

"What church ceremony?"

"Remember Saint Oswald's? We learnt about it in school."

"The place with the old font?"

I nodded.

"Oh, Tess, I'm so sorry."

"Don't be." I chuckled at the ridiculousness of everything. "We didn't organise that ourselves either. Grace did. And just like Mum, without telling us."

My sister covered her mouth, clearly trying not to laugh.

"Two dresses, two venues, and two interfering mothers," I said. "Aren't I the lucky one?"

Noise coming from the kitchen suddenly caught our attention.

"You *are* kidding me!" Ryan said, his excited proclamation filtering down the garden. "No way!"

"Sounds like someone's having fun," Sal said.

"Want to join them?" I asked. Knowing I couldn't hide away forever, I supposed it was as good a time as any to show my face.

She wrinkled her nose. "Beats being miserable out here."

"Come on then," I said.

We rose to our feet and headed to the house. Entering, India sat rolling her eyes at Leo and Ryan who laughed at something they were watching on India's phone. An enthused voice emanated from the screen.

"Isn't that...?" Convinced I recognised who it belonged to, I looked to my sister for confirmation.

She stared back at me, as if unable to believe it herself. "It can't be."

Clocking our entrance, Ryan hailed us over. "You've got to see this."

Leo looked up too. His smile faded and leaving the fun behind, he came to join me. "Everything okay?" he asked, tentative.

Sal gave me a look of reassurance, before heading over to Ryan.

"It seems that daughter of ours and your father have been keeping secrets," Ryan said, as she approached. "I caught her watching this."

"Everything's fine. I just needed some time out. To calm down," I said in answer to Leo's question.

Closing his eyes for a second, relief swept over his face. "I honestly thought you might call off the wedding."

I scoffed. "I can't say I didn't think about it."

Leo looked hurt and I immediately felt guilty for being so blunt.

"Don't worry." I leaned up and kissed his cheek. "It'll take more than Mum's antics to make me do that."

Leo smiled. "Glad to hear it. Come on." Taking my hand, he pulled me towards the others. "We could both do with a laugh right now. Take a look at this."

Focusing on the video, my eyes widened. I put a hand up to my chest at the sight of Dad and another man stood on a train station platform. Despite the pouring rain, the two of them were full of excited anticipation and kept talking over each other. I leaned in for a closer look. "Who's the other chap?"

"That's Hugo," Leo said. "Marianne's husband."

"He looks quite a character," Sal said.

Leo chuckled. "They're a great couple. Both as eccentric as each other."

"What *are* they doing?" I asked staring at the screen.

"This is the start of our day chasing the 201 Thumper," Dad said.

I turned to Leo, confused. "And what does he mean by a Thumper?"

"You'll see," Ryan said.

"Here she is!" Hugo called out. "In all her beauty."

I took in Dad and Hugo's excitement. They didn't seem to notice the torrential weather as they laughed and cheered. Engine noise threatened to drown out their voices, as the camera cut from the two men to a long green passenger train. Dad and Hugo could hardly contain themselves as the so-called 201 Thumper rolled by. "I can't believe Dad's a..." I laughed. "There I was, thinking he and Hugo were old work colleagues."

"I've never seen Edward so animated," Ryan said.

Sal shook her head. "Look at the state of him."

Dad was soaked. His hair lay flattened thanks to the rain and droplets of water dripped off the end of his nose. He carried a sodden rucksack which I didn't doubt contained sandwiches and a flask and as he and Hugo suddenly sprang into action, I realised Ryan was right. This was not the father I was used to. "He looks so happy." I turned to Leo. "Did you know about this?"

"Not for definite, but I had an idea. Hugo and I *are* building a track in his garden."

"A railway track?"

"With its very own platform."

"Wow! I guess that explains all the tonne bags." I returned my attention to the screen.

"Now we're rushing off to the coast to catch it again," Hugo said, as the two men raced toward the station exit. "It's going to be a Top Gear challenge," he said, as they charged across the car park to their vehicle. "But we'll do our best."

The video suddenly cut to a different platform.

"Here we are," Dad said, still smiling. "With seconds, just seconds, to spare." The 201 Thumper could be heard in the distance and Dad's attention was diverted when it came into view. "Whoa!" he called out, as it passed him by for a second time.

"Can I have my phone back now, please?" India said. Much to everyone else's disappointment, she reached over and grabbed it. Ignoring our protests she shut down the video, preventing us from seeing any more footage.

"I was enjoying that," Ryan said.

"Not as much as Dad was," Sal said. "No wonder Mum told us all he'd taken up golf."

"Oh, yeah," Ryan said. "Ha! It would seem Patricia Cavendish has been telling fibs."

I thought back to all the times Dad's alleged new pastime had come up in conversation and realising mine and Leo's wedding preparations hadn't affected Mum's neurons in the slightest, I smiled knowingly. "She does have a *tell* though."

"Does she?" Ryan asked.

"Oh yes. The woman can't lie to save her life."

"Tell me more," Ryan said.

"Whenever the subject of golf comes up, she gets this twitch, here." I touched the skin underneath my right eye. "Like a tic." I let out a laugh. "She'd never make a poker player."

A mischievous smile spread across Ryan's face. "Imagine the fun we can all have with this."

CHAPTER 43

"*H*ave you spoken to Mum yet?" my sister asked.

As Sal glanced out of the passenger door window and India slouched in the back, headphones on listening to music, I sat behind the wheel trying to concentrate on the road. It was a glorious summer evening and with the three of us on our way to Marianne's to talk wedding, matron of honour, and bridesmaid dresses, the last person I wanted to think about was my mother. My feelings about her were still raw and discussing her behaviour would, no doubt, have spoiled the night ahead. "Nope," I replied.

"Tess, you get married in just over two months. You're going to have to resolve things at some point. And when are Leo's parents landing? We're all supposed to be meeting up, remember?"

I bristled. "How can I forget?" I felt Sal's eyes on me, but I refused to get drawn in. "How about we talk about where we're going instead? Marianne did, after all, work with *the* Zane Rafferty. To be honest, I'm surprised you can think about anything else."

"It's called prioritising." Sal fidgeted in her seat, clearly trying to play it cool. "What do you think I am? Some sort of fan girl?"

I smiled as I recalled my sister's swooning back in the day, and as we continued our drive, no matter her denials, I knew that was exactly what Sal was.

It didn't take long for Marianne and Hugo's farmhouse to come into view and slowing the car, I brought it to a standstill.

"You mean we're here?" Sal said. "Already?" Springing to life, she reached for the rear-view mirror and twisted it round so she could see herself. "Do I look okay?" she asked, titivating with her hair. She glanced over at the property. "Oh my word, is that her?"

"What was that you said about not being a fan girl?"

Busy watering the flower beds, Marianne wore yet another kaftan and looking as colourful as ever, she paused in her task to give us a smile and a wave.

"You excited about this?" Sal asked India.

As we all alighted the vehicle, my sister tried to smooth down her daughter's hair.

"Not as much as you," India replied, wriggling away.

"To have a dress designed and made by a woman who worked with *the* Zane Rafferty," Sal said then sighed. "We are so lucky."

As we made our way up the garden path, I couldn't deny my own nervous anticipation. Mum's and Grace's wedding dresses might have provided Marianne with swathes of fabric, but I'd yet to learn if any of them were usable.

Marianne put down her watering can and gave me the warmest of hugs. "And who do we have here?" Letting go of me, she turned to the others.

"This is Sal," I said.

Stood there wearing a demented grin, my sister curtsied, an action I would never have believed had I not seen it with my own eyes.

"Pleased to meet you," Marianne said. Evidently as surprised by the gesture as I was, she gave me a discreet look of confusion.

"Sal's a big Zane Rafferty fan," I said.

"Ah, that explains it."

"And this is my niece, India," I said, moving on.

Marianne's eyes settled on India's fringe and I cringed, knowing that between my prior overconfidence, Sal's bended knee, and India's dodgy haircut, the three of us certainly knew how to create a first impression.

"So, you're Tess's bridesmaid?"

India fast nodded. Appearing as starstruck as her mother, she couldn't seem to take her eyes off Marianne.

"I can see this is going to be an interesting evening," Marianne said, laughing to herself as she led the way around to the back of the house.

I took the opportunity to give my sister a nudge, willing her to sort herself out.

What? she mouthed, as we followed Marianne into the kitchen.

"Wow," Sal said. Immediately struck by the photo of our host and Zane Rafferty, she went in for a closer look. "You really are fashion royalty."

Marianne gave an affectionate smile. "Him, maybe. Me, not so much."

"What was he like? As a person, I mean?"

Marianne joined my sister and while the two them talked all things Zane, India continued to be mesmerised by our host. I appreciated why. Marianne was confident and charismatic. She wasn't like anyone *I'd* ever met before, let alone a young girl like my niece.

Leaving them to their chat, my eyes fell on the dining table where the two wedding gowns had been sorted into neat piles. Not just according to differing fabrics, I noted, but also according to the type of panel. I ran my fingers over a stack of chiffon. The dresses themselves might have been ugly by modern standards, but there was no denying the materials used were gorgeous.

"They certainly liked their voluminosity back in the day," Marianne said, appearing at my side. She gave me a cheeky smile. "Luckily for us." She headed to the kettle and reaching for the teapot, set about making us all a drink.

"So, we can definitely do something with all this?" I asked.

"We can indeed."

My heart skipped a beat. It seemed my dress woes really were over.

"Would you like to see the designs I came up with?"

"Yes, please," I said, suddenly nervous.

She turned to India. "I've drawn a couple for you to choose from, young lady."

"Really?" India's eyes lit up. "Did you hear that, Mum? I get a choice."

Tea made, Marianne headed to the dresser and opening a drawer, pulled out a pencil, pad, and a tape measure. Rejoining us, she hung the tape measure around her neck and placed her other two items on the kitchen counter. "Who wants to go first?"

I took in India's eagerness, and I indicated she go ahead, prompting Marianne to flip to the relevant pages.

"This one has a scoop neck and asymmetrical hemline," Marianne said. "See?" She held up her sketchpad revealing both the back and front of the design she'd come up with.

"That's beautiful," Sal said.

"The snug fit of the sleeveless bodice works really well with the flared high-low skirt, which I think will highlight your silhouette perfectly." Marianne smiled at my niece. "What do you think?"

"I really like it," India said.

Marianne turned to a different page. "The next one has more of a V-neck and is the same length all the way round. It features a cross-pleated bodice and has a sash which is tied into a bow at the back. It's got short flutter sleeves made from some of the sheer fabric we have, and the skirt is chiffon, which cascades down to your ankles. It's more of a romantic look than the first design."

India pointed to the second drawing. "I think I'd like this one."

Marianne crinkled up her face with a smile. "That one's my favourite too."

"And mine," Sal said, although in my view she'd have said that no matter which of the two her daughter chose.

Marianne turned to me. "I know it's not customary for bridesmaids and matrons of honour to wear the same colour as the bride, but with the fabric being the age it is, I'm loath to try to dye it. I wouldn't want anything to go wrong."

"I'm fine with that," I said.

"Are you ready to see yours, Sal?" Marianne asked my sister.

"Am I," Sal replied.

Marianne turned the page again. "I've gone for a scoop neck in your case and an A-line silhouette that drapes from the waist all the way down to the floor. As you can see, I'll be using some of the fancier more detailed fabrics for the top half, and some of the plainer longer lengths for the bottom."

"It's stunning," my sister said. "And I love the short sleeves."

"You know what the best thing about this dress is?" Marianne asked.

Sal shook her head.

"It's got pockets."

"No! That's fantastic." Sal gave her daughter a nudge. "Did you hear that, India? Mine's got pockets."

"Now for the wedding dress." Marianne looked at me, her eyes wide. "Are you ready?"

As Marianne, yet again, flipped over the page, I took a sharp intake of breath.

"As you can see, I've followed your lead and gone with a vintage vibe. It's tea length like the one in your sketch and has the clean-cut V-neck you were hoping for. But if you look at the chest on mine, this one isn't quite as deep."

"This looks great."

"It's got sheer half-sleeves, with lace appliqué on the bodice and the skirt is A-line, which gradually widens from a pleated waist. And whereas the other two dresses are mainly chiffon, this one's made from tulle." Description over with, Marianne awaited my response.

"I think I'm going to cry," I said.

"Never mind *think*," Sal said, forced to wipe her eyes. "I don't think I've ever seen such a gorgeous wedding dress."

"We're all happy then?" Marianne asked.

Sal, India and I nodded.

"Wonderful." Marianne whipped her tape measure from around her neck. "Now I need to take all your measurements."

"Are you sure you'll have enough time to make all these?" I asked. Conscious the wedding was fast approaching, I didn't want Marianne feeling under pressure.

"For an old pro like me? You're joking, aren't you?"

Again, my eyes filled with tears. "I can't thank you enough, Marianne. When I think of the mess I was in... I honestly don't know what I'd have done without you."

CHAPTER 44

"*J*t's good to see you happy again," Leo said.

"It's good to *feel* happy again," I replied.

As we stood at the sink washing and drying the dishes from our evening meal, we both knew the reason behind my good mood. I hadn't stopped smiling since Marianne had revealed her wedding dress design. She wasn't simply turning the dress of my dreams into a reality; she'd transformed my vision into something even more beautiful. "I'd like to give Marianne a gift," I said. "You know, to say thank you."

"Maybe you could throw her something? From one creative to another?"

I paused mid plate dry, wondering if I was brave enough to do that. Marianne had worked with one of the biggest names in her field. In mine, I didn't have anywhere near that kind of reputation. I didn't want to risk insulting the woman by acting like I was her equal. "You think?" I thought back to my prior overconfidence. Having embarrassed myself already, I was in no rush to repeat the experience.

"I do, Tess. I've never known you make anything that hasn't

come straight from the heart. And if I can see the love that goes into your work, Marianne will too."

"When you put it like that." I stretched up to kiss Leo's cheek, appreciating the faith he had in me. "How can I not?" I picked up yet another plate. "You know, I might even be coming around to the idea of saying my vows in front of a room full of strangers."

Leo looked at me, surprised, although after the fuss I'd made, I couldn't blame him.

"Let's just say a gown like mine should be shown off." I came over all serious. "Which reminds me, did you cancel Saint Oswald's?"

"I did. And you'll be pleased to know, Reverend Joseph was very understanding. He appreciated that weddings bring out the best and *worst* in people. I got the impression our issues are nothing compared to what he's seen."

I found that hard to believe. "What is it about families? You'd think two people getting married would pull everyone together."

"Does this mean you're ready to sort things out with Patricia?" Leo asked, eyebrows raised.

My smile froze. "I walked straight into that, didn't I?"

Leo chuckled, while I sighed.

"I suppose I'm going to have to at some point," I said, as I continued drying the dishes.

"Preferably before Mum and Dad get here?" Leo said.

"No pressure then?" I said, mocking. I paused in my actions. "When do they land?"

"In a couple of days."

Having hoped to delay the inevitable for as long as I could, it was good to know I had at least a little breathing space before dealing with Mum.

"Which is why…" Leo said.

"Yoo hoo!"

I cocked my head. "What's she doing here?"

Leo suddenly came over all guilty looking.

I glared at him. "You invited her?"

He nodded.

"How could you? Talk about going behind my back."

"It's only me," Mum called out.

Leo put the last of the dishes on the draining board. "Someone had to make the first move." He tipped the water from the bowl into the sink. "And it didn't look like either of you two were going to do it."

"But still."

Leo looked at me, his eyes pleading. "Come on, Tess. I couldn't just sit around and do nothing. Wedding or no wedding, it's not like I'm going anywhere, and Mum and Dad would still want to meet your lot. If you can't do this for yourself, or even for my parents, then, please, do it for me."

"Do I have a choice?" I asked. In all the time I'd known Leo, he had never asked much of me, and I told myself that, as such, the least I could do was listen to what my mother had to say. "Okay," I said, my voice low. "But she better be here to apologise."

"Thank you."

Mum appeared in the doorway. "Can I come in?"

I turned to face Mum, surprised to see her on her own. "No Dad?"

"No, erm, he's busy tonight."

"Playing golf, is he?" As the tic appeared under Mum's eye, I knew my question was mean, but after what Mum had done, I couldn't resist.

Leo whispered in my ear. "Play nice."

The tic sped up, before Mum waved my question away. "I'm not here to talk about your father." She sat down at the table and gathered herself. "I'm here to say sorry." Her regard went from me to Leo. "To both of you."

Leo set about making a pot of tea, while I took a seat opposite Mum. "Go on."

"You were right to be upset." She looked down at her hands

while she spoke. "You made it clear that you wanted a small wedding, and I didn't listen."

"No, you didn't," I said.

"I should never have invited all those extra guests."

"No, you shouldn't."

"Or booked Gregbrook Manor without discussing it with you first."

I scoffed. "You got that right."

Mum, at last, lifted her head. She stared at me direct. "You're not making this easy."

"No, Mum. I'm not."

Leo placed the tea tray down in front of us, before lowering himself into the chair next to me. "Thank you, Patricia. Your apology means a lot." He gave me a pointed look. "Doesn't it, Tess?"

"Yes," I said, my voice quiet.

"Pardon?" Leo said.

"Yes," I repeated, with a glower.

"Although this isn't just about you going rogue, Mum," I said, needing her to understand things from our perspective. "It's all the extra work you've created. Leo was meant to be doing the flowers, now we're going to have to draft someone in. In the middle of wedding season. Then there's–"

"They're included," Mum said.

"What?" I frowned at the interruption.

"The flowers. They're included in the wedding package. All you have to do is decide what you want."

I shook my head. "That's not the point I'm making, Mum. What I'm trying–"

"So is the wedding breakfast. Of course, you weren't around to decide what you wanted, so I had no choice but to…"

Mum's voice trailed off into a mumble, so I didn't properly catch the end of her sentence. "You had to what?"

She mumbled again.

I wasn't stupid. I knew she was telling me she'd chosen the menu for our wedding reception. However, clinging onto the remnants of my earlier good humour, I was determined not to get into another argument. I took a deep breath and gathered myself. "Mum," I said, keeping my cool. "If we'd wanted everything organised for us, don't you think we'd have agreed to take on Wendy?"

I considered all Mum's interference those last months. From her mood boards to her trying to make us hire a wedding planner, to me wearing her dress, to her deciding our ultimate venue...

As much as I hadn't wanted to see it before, I had to wonder if India had been right when she'd said Mum and Dad weren't married. Maybe me and Leo getting hitched was Mum's opportunity to have her own dream wedding, albeit vicariously.

As I opened my mouth to ask, I couldn't bring myself to do it. Like Leo had said, his parents were due to land, and if my suspicions proved correct, risking another falling out wouldn't be fair to Leo or them.

"I know I keep saying it, but I don't mean to cause a problem. I simply want you to have the best wedding ever," Mum said. "You have to believe that."

I couldn't deny her sincerity, and telling myself that India had to be wrong, I dismissed my parents' marital status altogether. "I just don't want any more surprises, Mum," I said, making a point of keeping my voice stern. "You do know that, don't you?"

Mum nodded. "I do."

"As long as I've made myself clear."

"Oh, you have." Mum smiled. "Does this mean we can talk about Gregbrook Manor now?"

Convinced she hadn't heard one iota of what I'd said, I stared at her, aghast. Lost for words, I turned to Leo for help, but he simply shrugged, as if telling me I'd done everything I could. I scoffed at the situation, resigned to the fact that while Mum's response might not have been perfect, it was probably the best I was going to get.

$\mathcal{W}$hile I sat reading, with my feet up on the sofa, Otis lay stretched out on the rug. It might have been a couple of hours off, but I knew I should be getting ready for the big dinner. For me, bathing, doing something with my unruly hair, and putting on make-up took time, and that was before I got round to deciding what to wear. Leo's parents were due to meet my family that evening, and I wanted to look my best for the occasion. However, every time I thought about it, my nerves hit, and I couldn't bring myself to move.

Otis and I cocked our heads at the sound of the front door opening and closing. "That didn't take long?" I said, as Leo appeared in the lounge. Folding the corner of my page down so I didn't lose my place, I uncurled my legs from under me and gave Leo my full attention. "I thought you'd be ages yet."

"And I thought you'd be in the bath."

I indicated my book. "I got to a good bit and couldn't put it down."

"I left Mum and Dad at the hotel." He dropped his keys onto the coffee table. "I didn't see the point in hanging around when we're seeing them later."

"I can't believe they chose to stay somewhere else." After we'd guested at theirs, I'd hoped to return the hospitality. "They were more than welcome here."

"Which is exactly what I told them, but they wouldn't have it. Apparently, we have enough to think about with the wedding coming up, without playing host."

I let out a laugh. Thanks to Mum's intervention and Gregbrook Manor's extensive wedding package, that wasn't strictly the case. Aside of my wedding, India's bridesmaid and Sal's matron of honour dresses, along with Leo's suit, everything else seemed to be covered. "Our only major task is to sort out the marriage notification," I said. "I would like to speak to the venue organiser first though, to make sure we're happy with everything."

"Sounds good to me."

While Leo had got his head around our surprise all-inclusive wedding, I continued to have reservations. Yes, on the one hand, it meant I could get rid of all the lists and not worry about blue ticks. But on the other, I continued to struggle with the fact that we weren't getting the day we'd hoped for. I screwed up my face in anticipation. "What did your parents say about us cancelling Father Joseph and Saint Oswald's?"

"Dad was fine, but Mum was disappointed."

An upset mother-in-law-to-be was all I needed.

"But she understood," Leo said.

"Really?" I straightened myself up again, relieved to hear that.

Leo shook his head. "Nope. Not at all."

I grabbed a cushion and threw it at him.

Leo laughed as he dodged out of its way. "I'm just glad the pressure's off. Instead of stressing, we can enjoy the run-up to the wedding." He plonked himself down next to me. "I did feel a bit bad telling her though. She'd set her heart on us having a church service."

I pictured the evening ahead. Mum celebrating her

Gregbrook Manor victory, while Grace commiserated her Saint Oswald loss. It seemed that despite having everything sorted, our wedding continued to cause problems. As if I wasn't dreading the family introductions enough. "Tonight will be okay, won't it?" I asked, looking to Leo for reassurance. "Everyone will get on, won't they?"

"Tonight will be fine. Mum might be unhappy now, but she's not one to hold grudges. Honestly, by the time we get to the restaurant, she'll be over it."

CHAPTER 46

"You did tell everyone the table is booked under your name?" I asked, as Leo and I drove to the restaurant.

"I did," Leo replied.

"And the restaurant people know exactly how many of us there are and where to seat everyone?"

"They do."

"Because you know what my lot are like. They're not always the easiest people to organise. They'll cause chaos as a group if they're not herded properly."

Knowing exactly what I meant, Leo smiled.

"Oh, and you wrote down the precise name of the restaurant for Mum and Dad, didn't you?" I pictured my parents, Sal and Ryan sat in one establishment, while Grace and Bill waited for us in another. "Remember the occasion..."

"Tess," Leo said, interrupting me. "Stop worrying. Everyone involved knows what they're meant to be doing, where they're meant to be, and at what time."

Arriving at our destination, Leo pulled up in the car park. Turning off the engine and releasing his keys from the ignition, he turned to look at me. "Please, try to relax. You really are panicking over nothing." He put a hand on mine. "Trust me. As evenings go, this one will be perfect."

I smiled. As far as I was concerned *perfection* was a bit of a push. Then again Leo had always been a glass half-full kind of person. "You're right," I said, deciding to go with Leo's positive flow. "The Cavendishes know how important tonight is. Of course they'll be on their best behaviour."

"Exactly," Leo said, as we climbed out of the car.

"How do I look?" I asked. Not usually one for dresses, I wore a green boho maxi number with three quarter sleeves and tie cuffs. It had a floaty full skirt and I paired it with a pair of flat sandals.

"Gorgeous as always." Leo took my hand. "Ready?"

I took a deep breath and nodded. "Let's do this."

Entering the restaurant, Leo gave the front of house our name while I glanced around. I could see why Leo had chosen it; the dining area was gorgeous. The space's use of raw materials, old refurbished tables and chairs, and warm lighting gave the eatery a cosy atmosphere.

"Tess," Mum called out.

I heard her before I saw her.

"Over here," she said, waving her arm in the air.

Seeing that Mum, Dad, Sal, and Ryan were already seated and waiting, Leo and I made our way over.

Leo squeezed my hand as we walked. "Here's to a great evening," he said and as the Cavendishes stood up to greet us, it was hugging all round before Leo's and my bum got anywhere near a chair.

"No India?" I asked.

"Ryan's parents have taken her to the cinema," Sal said.

Having already ordered drinks, Dad poured us a glass of wine, while Mum checked her watch. "Someone's running late," she said.

I flashed her a look.

"I'm just saying. Leo's parents are new in town. For all anyone knows they could have got lost."

Refusing to let my nerves get the better of me, I told myself to calm down and that Mum had a point.

"Is there anything you can tell us about your parents before they get here, Leo?" Mum asked. "I'm thinking if we have something in common, that might make the conversation flow a bit easier."

"Hopefully, Bill will be a fellow golfer, eh, Ed?" Ryan said. "You can compare drivers and putters and whatever else you *sporty* types use."

While Mum's twitch kicked in, I didn't think I'd ever seen Dad so uncomfortable.

"The food here looks good," Mum said. Grabbing a couple of menus, she passed one to Dad. "Doesn't it, Edward?"

Watching them, the rest of us tried not to laugh. I shook my head at Ryan's naughtiness.

"It certainly does," Dad said. Following Mum's lead, he scanned the meal choices.

It was obvious to everyone at the table that Dad knew as little about the game as the rest of us and seeing his discomfort, I felt sorry for him. In my view, he should've just owned up to being a trainspotter. As hobbies go, his might not have been the coolest of choices but he shouldn't let Mum railroad him into silence simply to save her embarrassment. Then again, I supposed the woman was an expert. No matter my protests, she'd found a way to railroad me too.

With his eyes on the door, Leo's smile grew. "Looks like they're here." He waved to his parents as they entered the restaurant.

I almost failed to recognise my future in-laws. They'd been transformed. Unlike the country bumpkins I'd first met, Bill and Grace appeared distinguished. Bill's hair had been tamed with Brylcreem, and he wore his suit, shirt, and tie well. Combining classic and contemporary, Grace's royal blue dress was stunning. With its midi hemline and a statement tie belt that emphasised her waist, the woman oozed style. Her perfect make-up and effortless wispy chignon finished the ensemble perfectly.

Clearly thinking the same thing when it came to Grace, Dad's eyes lit up before Mum gave him a scowl and a nudge that quickly brought him back into line.

Clocking our parents' interaction, Sal laughed, while I cringed, hoping it wasn't a sign of things to come. The Cavendishes could be *interesting* when they wanted to be and although they were good people at heart, they didn't always do themselves justice. Come the end of the night I only hoped Grace and Bill weren't left wondering what kind of family their son was marrying into.

We all rose to our feet as my future in-laws neared and Leo introduced everyone one by one.

"Sorry we're late," Bill said. "You can blame this one." He indicated his wife.

"Cheeky." Grace turned her attention to the group. "It's been so long since we've had an evening out, I'd forgotten how long it takes to get ready."

Bill turned to the rest of us. "Plus, she insisted we stop off for a drink on the way."

Grace threw her husband a look. "Well, we're here now and it's lovely to meet you all, at last."

As everyone sat down, Bill turned to Leo and discreetly mouthed an apology.

"Can you believe these two are finally getting married?" Grace said to Mum.

"I know. Isn't it exciting?" Mum replied.

"We're really looking forward to Tess joining our family," Grace said.

I felt myself blush.

"We feel the same about Leo," Mum replied.

So far, so good, I thought.

"Ah, but does he feel the same about us?" Sal asked. Putting her glass to her lips, she winked at Leo.

"I'd make a run for it, mate. Before it's too late," Ryan said.

"It's such a shame about the church ceremony though, isn't it?" Grace said, at the same time swatting out her napkin.

I looked to Leo. To say he'd said his mother didn't hold grudges, she'd dropped her disappointment into the conversation pretty swiftly.

"Church service?" Mum said.

Leo opened his mouth to explain, but his mother jumped in first.

"Sorry, I thought you knew."

"Knew what?" Mum looked to me, confused.

"That I'd arranged a proper service with Reverend Joseph," Grace said.

"Proper?" Mum said, her hackles rising.

"Which had to be cancelled because you'd booked some fancy manor house?"

Mum took a deep breath, clearly trying to remain calm.

"Don't get me wrong," Grace continued. "These civil ceremonies are all very nice, it's just a shame their union won't be taking place in the eyes of God."

I leaned into Leo. "Please tell me what's happening here."

"So they are no longer two, but one flesh," Grace said, with a flourish. "What therefore *God* has joined together, let no man separate… Matthew, Chapter 19, Verse 6."

As Mum turned to Leo, I couldn't tell if she was embarrassed or confused by Grace's outburst. "You never said you came from religious stock, Leo."

Again, he tried to speak.

"Should he have?" Grace said, drawing Mum's attention back to her.

Oh, Lordy, I thought.

Sal reached for a menu. "So, what's everyone having?" She smiled broadly. "I don't know about you lot, but I'm starving."

"Me too," Ryan said.

Everyone except the two mothers followed suit and began exaggerated perusals over what to eat.

"It's going to be a hard choice," Bill said. "Everything looks so good." He tried to interest his wife, but she was having none of it.

"And Saint Oswald's has such a lovely font. The oldest in Europe if I'm not mistaken," Grace said. "Eh, Tess?"

Mum flashed me a look, daring me to take Grace's side.

"What do you fancy, love?" Dad asked. He offered Mum a menu, but she waved it away.

"Then you'll be pleased to hear that Gregbrook Manor has a wonderful French fountain," she said instead.

"I can't believe they're both behaving like this," I said to Leo.

"And with such politeness," he replied with sarcasm. "I dread to think what they're going to be like once they get to know each other."

My stare went from mum to Grace and back again. "There must be a way to stop them."

"I don't think there is."

"Well, you may have got your way over the ceremony," Grace said, upping the antics. "But I have the wonderful honour of *your* daughter wearing *my* beautiful wedding gown."

"Oh no." Mum let out a laugh, as if she'd never heard anything so ridiculous. "I think you'll find she's wearing mine."

Both women looked my way.

"Tess?" Grace said.

I swallowed hard.

"Well?" Mum said.

CHAPTER 47

*L*eo and I sat at the kitchen table and like me, Leo seemed to be using the silence to get his head around the previous evening's events. We'd tried talking about things as soon as we landed home from the restaurant, but it had been the wrong time.

Not usually ones to snipe at each other, we'd each felt an unreasonable need to defend our respective mother's behaviour. I recalled how things between us ultimately descended into an argument. Instead of getting an apology from the real culprits, we spent the rest of the night saying sorry to each other.

"I have to wonder if Mum was drunk," Leo finally said. "I've never seen her like that before." He took a sip of coffee. "Dad did say they'd stopped off for one on the way to meet us."

"Goodness knows what my mum's excuse was," I replied. Patricia Cavendish might have started out controlling her tongue, but as soon as the subject of wedding dresses came up, she let it get a whole lot looser. "On the plus side," I said.

Leo looked at me like I'd lost the plot. "You think there's a positive to all this?"

"I was thinking about the long list of extra wedding guests

we've acquired. With a packed ceremony and reception, it'll be easier to keep them apart." I scoffed. "Hopefully they'll be too busy mingling to even think about going for round two."

"As long as we don't have ringside seats. They can do what they want."

A loud knock at the front door interrupted our conversation. With both of us wondering who had come a calling, Leo shrugged, before rising to his feet and going to find out.

Hearing voices, I cocked my head, straining to hear. But as the hushed tones continued, I couldn't decipher a word.

Reappearing in the kitchen doorway, Leo gave me a warning look, before stepping aside to let Grace and Bill through.

Seeing them stood there, I immediately felt nervous. Having experienced enough disputes of late, I certainly didn't want to find myself in the middle of another.

"What a lovely house," Grace said, taking in my somewhat-eclectic design choices. She turned her attention onto me. "And in such a lovely spot."

"We like it," I said. I knew Leo's parents hadn't come all the way from town to talk about life in the Yorkshire Dales, and refusing to engage in any more small talk, I waited for Grace to say what was really on her mind.

The woman looked to Bill, who gave her what appeared to be an encouraging nod. "Can we?" Grace said, indicating the empty chairs at the table.

"Of course," I said. "Please do."

"I'll make more coffee," Leo said, as his parents took their seats.

"No," Grace said to her son. "It's all right."

Leo halted.

"We're not stopping. The taxi's waiting to take us to the train station."

"Oh," Leo said, his disappointment evident.

"It's nothing to do with you two," Bill said, as if needing to clarify. "We'd already arranged to nip up to Cumbria. Before all this… Well, you know. And having let one son down." He gave his wife a pointed look. "It wouldn't be right to let the other one down too." He smiled at Leo, who, in return, seemed to appreciate the explanation.

"And I needed to apologise before we left," Grace said. "My behaviour last night was terrible."

"Yes, Mum. It was," Leo said.

"I don't know what came over me." She paused. "Actually I do." Grace let out a long, despondent sigh. "A heart at peace gives life to the body, but envy rots the bones. Proverbs, Chapter 14, Verse 30."

Leo shook his head as if the last thing he wanted to hear was scripture. "Meaning?"

"Meaning," Grace said. Her shoulders slumped. "I was jealous. I felt like you were favouring Tess's mum over me."

I almost laughed. Grace couldn't have been further from the truth if she'd tried.

"I was so looking forward to your little church wedding," Grace continued. "In fact, I hadn't realised how much, until you said it wasn't happening. And all because Patricia…"

I shifted in my seat. It was one thing me and my sister being critical of Mum, but something else to hear another person talk bad of her.

"You're talking like the woman went above your head," Leo said, before his mum could finish. "As if Patricia booked Gregbrook Manor simply to spite you. Tess's mum didn't even know about the Saint Oswald's gig. Something she made pretty clear."

Grace put a hand up. "I know. And I see that now. Whereas last night, it wouldn't have mattered what she said, I just saw red. You have to understand, to me marriage is a holy sacrament."

"Which is fine," Leo said. "But as much as I try to respect you and your faith, Mum, you need to respect the way I choose to live my life. Along with the people in it, and that includes Patricia."

Grace nodded. "I understand."

Watching their interaction, I wished my family could be more like that. Grace didn't only give her son the opportunity to speak his mind, she appeared to properly listen. Whenever I tried to talk to my mum, she'd either cut me off and start talking herself, or she'd nod in all the right places, before going off and doing her own thing anyway.

"And, Tess, I do apologise. Wholeheartedly. To you and your mum."

Able to see she meant that, I gave Grace an appreciative smile.

A car horn beeped. "Looks like it's time to go," Bill said.

Grace rose to her feet. "Is a hug goodbye allowed?"

Leo's expression relaxed. "Of course it is," he said, embracing his mum.

I stood, as Grace turned her attention to me. "Again, please tell your mum I'm sorry."

"I will," I said, hugging Grace in return. "And thank you for coming today. It means a lot." I indicated Leo, who'd thrown his arms around his dad. "To your son and me."

As his parents made their exit, Leo and I accompanied them to the front door.

"We'll see you both at the wedding," Bill said.

"Although I'm sure we'll speak before then," Grace said.

"We'll video call," Leo said.

After watching them climb into the taxi, Leo and I stood there waving as the vehicle pulled away.

"One down, one to go," Leo said, as it finally disappeared.

I let out a laugh.

"What?"

"You don't really think we'll get an apology from *my* mum, do you?"

"Why wouldn't we?"

217

"Because that would make two in the same week. Her first was hard enough."

"And?"

I stretched up and kissed Leo's cheek. "That's one of the things I love about you. Your unwavering optimism." Leaving Leo stood there, I continued to chuckle as I headed back inside.

"Patricia will tell us she's sorry," he said, calling after me.

"No, she won't."

"Tenner says she will."

I shook my head and smiled. "You're on."

CHAPTER 48

"These really are beautiful," Leo said. "The colours really pop."

I'd spent days in my workshop hand-painting a pair of bisque fired platters for Marianne. Taking her love of colour as my starting point, I'd used reds, blues, and yellows to create an abstract floral design employing a mishmash of shapes and shades. After dipping and a final firing, I knew when I took them out of the kiln that they looked good and as I bandaged each one in bubble wrap, I hoped Marianne liked them as much as I did.

The sound of a vehicle pulling up on the drive caught my attention. "That'll be Sal," I said. My sister honked the horn, as if telling me to get a move on, and placing the platters in a box, I picked the whole thing up and grabbed my bag. I took a deep breath, ready to go and see my dress for the very first time.

"It'll be stunning," Leo said.

I smiled. "I know." I moved to leave, but Leo put his hand out to stop me.

"Is everything okay?" he asked.

I nodded. "Of course. Why wouldn't it be?" After kissing his cheek, I headed down the hall and out to the car.

Placing the box on the back seat next to India, I chuckled at the sight of her. Earphones in listening to something on her mobile, India wore a cerise kaftan, with a matching headscarf that knotted at the side and hid her lack of a fringe. With a tape measure hanging round her neck, Marianne had clearly made an impression on the girl. "Dressmaker-come-pattern-designer?" I asked Sal.

"Oh, yes," she replied.

As I climbed into the front, Sal waited for me to fasten my seat belt before pulling away. "So how's things? More importantly, did you get an apology from Mum and Grace?"

My sister had a habit of getting straight to the point. "I meant to call and ask," she carried on. "But work's been so busy."

"Grace, yes. She came to the house the next morning."

Sal looked impressed.

"You should have seen her, Sal. She really was sorry. And the way she and Leo talked it out. Did you know, there are mothers out there who actually listen to their offspring?"

Sal smirked. "And Mum?"

"Not even a phone call. Complete radio silence."

Sal tutted and shook her head.

"She'll turn up when she's ready," I said. "To be honest, I'm glad she's stayed away. She's hit me with so many surprises these last few months. Each one bigger than the last. To the point, I don't think I can take any more. Every time I see her, I get this sense of dread in my stomach. Just in case she's about to drop another bombshell."

"The run up to this wedding of yours has certainly been eventful."

"Tell me about it. I don't get why she can't simply be happy for us. Instead of making everything about her. I'm convinced that's why she's not been round. She's sulking. Waiting for me to call her so she can be centre of attention again."

"How does Leo feel about it all?"

"He's handling things far better than me, as usual." I sighed. "I've given up talking to him about it."

Sal glanced my way, her face concerned. "I don't like the sound of that." My sister's unease grew. "Tess, are you all right?"

I looked back at her direct. "Truthfully? I don't think I am. I mean look at me. I'm on my way to try on the dress of my dreams and I don't feel anything. Despite its rough start, this wedding gown is the one thing that's gone right for me and it's like if I allow myself to get excited, then…" I let my voice trail off. I considered how much the wedding we were getting differed from the one we'd planned. "How did we get into this mess, Sal? Why didn't I put my foot down?"

"Probably because every time you did say something, you were told not to stress because people meant well."

I couldn't disagree. But neither could I deny any responsibility on my part. "It's my fault too. I should have listened to you and learnt how to properly say no once in a while."

Sal reached over and rubbed my arm. "Come on. Forget about Mum and everyone else. At least for now. Tonight's about you and I don't care what's going on, you deserve to enjoy it. You're seeing your dream wedding dress for the first time and I, for one, can't wait." She raised her eyebrows and smiled. "No matter what happens at your wedding, I promise you, you'll at least have a nice cake."

My expression relaxed into a smile. "Good to know." I knew my sister was right. That I should stop worrying about what might come next and focus on what matters. "So tell me. What does this cake entail?"

Sal spent the rest of the drive updating me on her plans. As Leo and I hadn't been able to narrow down which flavour to choose, she'd decided to use all the ones we'd tasted bar the Christmassy fruit cake.

"So, it'll have four tiers?" I asked, shocked.

Keeping her left hand on the wheel, Sal counted them out on her fingers. "Chocolate, lemon and elderflower, vanilla and raspberry, and white chiffon."

Recalling the taste of each one of them, my mouth began to water.

"Yes, four. And I thought I'd take your dress as inspiration and go for a vintage vibe. I'm thinking of an ivory or blush pink base with white royal icing over-piping. Using the Lambeth method."

"Which is?" Being a cake eater and not a cake maker, that meant nothing to me.

"It's used to create rows of intricate details. Scrolls and garlands, that type of thing. Creating a sense of depth and layering to the decoration. Lambeth cakes tend to be a bit more lavish in style and although they went out of fashion for a while, they're now *very* on trend." She smiled. "So, what do you think?"

"Isn't that a lot of work?"

"Only the best for you and Leo."

I smiled, appreciating her words. "In that case, it sounds perfect."

Sal flicked on the car indicator, before pulling up outside Marianne's farmhouse. Sal turned to look at me. "Time to check out these dresses."

CHAPTER 49

*W*e all climbed out of the car, and after retrieving the box from the back seat, headed up the path and round to the back of the property where Marianne was ready and waiting for us.

"Here you all are," she said. Her eyes fell on India. "Oh my word. It seems I have my own mini-me."

"I've decided to become a dressmaker," India said. "And a pattern designer for a big fashion house."

"And very pleased I am to hear that." Marianne winked at me and Sal. "If appearances are anything to go by, young lady, I'd say you'll make a proper career out of it."

India smiled, delighted by the compliment.

"These are for you," I said, handing over the box.

Marianne tilted her head. "Thank you. But a gift? You really didn't have to."

I felt anxious as I watched her place the box on the table.

Proceeding to open it, Marianne's eyes widened as she freed the platters of bubble wrap. "These are gorgeous. Look at the colours." Placing them side by side, she looked my way again. "Please tell me you made them."

"I did," I said. "My makers mark is underneath."

"I shall treasure them." Marianne gave me an appreciative hug, before gathering herself. "Now to business," she said, at the same time turning to India. "I think Aunt Tess should model her dress first. Don't you?"

India nodded.

Marianne smiled my way. "You ready?"

I too nodded, although after all the gown-related issues I couldn't deny I felt nervous.

She guided me from the kitchen into an inner hall. "You go and pop it on and I'll be up shortly. Upstairs, door straight ahead."

As I followed Marianne's directions, my heart rate picked up pace. There'd been so much stress surrounding this dress, I couldn't believe it was ready for me to try on. Reaching the door, I paused, wiping my hand down my jeans before turning the handle.

Stepping into Marianne's whitewashed bedroom, I found the space as bright and relaxing as the rest of the house. It was dominated by an oak-framed bed, made up with crisp white linen, sumptuous pillows and cushions, and a colourful floral eiderdown that had been folded over halfway down the mattress.

An old painting of a vase containing red, white, and orange flowers on a turquoise background hung above the headboard, while a long wooden seat leant against the foot. With its simple rustic bedside tables, antique pine drawers and wardrobes, and unfussy light fittings, everything looked perfect. Including my wedding dress.

My breath caught at the mere sight of it and I had to swallow. Hanging against a tall free-standing mirror, it was like a piece of art.

I took in its clean-cut V-neck, sheer half-sleeves, and full A-line skirt, before lifting my hand to touch the lace appliqué that sat on the bodice. Marianne's stitching was exquisite. "How did you do this?" I asked, mesmerised. The whole dress was an exact replica of Marianne's drawing. Pulling myself away, I began to undress so I could try it on, smiling at the sound of chatter as it filtered in through the open sash window.

"Does she know how talented she is?" Marianne asked Sal, clearly talking about my platters. "I mean, look at this design. These flowers."

I heard the smile in the woman's voice.

"I'm not sure I'll be able to use them they're so wonderful."

I couldn't believe a woman as gifted as Marianne was praising my work like that.

Turning my attention to the wedding gown, I carefully slipped it on. I filled my cheeks with air and exhaled, before turning to the mirror. As I eyed my reflection, I'd never looked so glamorous and I twisted and turned first one way and then the other to admire it from all angles. I gathered up my hair and wound it in a bun-like fashion on the top of my head. Letting it fall again, I stood there. Thanks to Marianne, I felt like a Hollywood star.

A gentle knock on the bedroom door interrupted my concentration and I turned to see Marianne pop her head in.

"Here, let me," she said, her arms out ready to finish zipping up the back as she entered. Marianne stood in silence for a moment staring at my reflection in the mirror. "So, what do you think?"

My smile grew. "It's stunning." Unable to help myself, I threw my arms around her and hugged her tight. "It's even more beautiful than I imagined. Thank you."

As I took in the gown once more, I suddenly felt overwhelmed. Marianne's dress was a shining light amongst the quagmire of stresses and strains. A tear fell down my cheek and not wanting to spoil the evening or burden Marianne with my problems, I quickly wiped it away in the hope that she hadn't seen.

"Tess," Marianne said. "What is it?"

"I'm sorry." I felt my cheeks redden. "I don't mean to cry."

"This isn't just about the dress, is it?"

I couldn't bring myself to answer.

Marianne sat down on the bed and patted the spot next to her. "Come on. Tell me."

As I began to open up, it was clear that Marianne wasn't only a fabulous dressmaker; she was a great listener, who seemed genuinely concerned about what I'd been going through. Not once did she interrupt me, she simply let my tears flow as I told her about how my and Leo's engagement had unleashed a monster in Mum.

Marianne shook her head in all the right places as I snivelled my way through the Gregbrook Manor debacle. And she tutted and sighed when I outlined how I'd never felt so out of control over anything. As Marianne became increasingly worried, I almost didn't tell her about the competition between Mum and Grace. But having started to properly let things out, I couldn't seem to stop.

"Oh, you poor love," Marianne said, when my tears finally ran out.

"So now you know why this dress makes me so happy. You made me exactly what I asked for, instead of deciding it for me."

"You know what I think?" Marianne said.

I shook my head.

"I think you should talk to your mum. Be honest. Tell her exactly what you've just told me. Because despite... How shall I put this? Her enthusiasm. She will understand."

"I have tried. It's getting her to listen that's the problem."

Marianne gave me a gentle smile. "Then try again."

CHAPTER 50

*L*eo and I sat in our back garden, a cafetière of strong coffee to hand. We yawned as we soaked up the sun, neither of us having had a great night's sleep. Worried about that morning's overdue and potentially difficult conversation with Mum, I'd tossed and turned for hours, which, in turn, had kept Leo awake. And while Leo looked as tired as I felt, Otis pootled about the flora and fauna, sulking on account of him having had to take his morning constitutional in the garden instead of enjoying a long ramble in the countryside.

Leo and I let out a sigh, picked up our cups and drank.

"How are you feeling?" he asked. "About talking to Patricia?"

"Nervous. Worried she'll take things the wrong way." I recalled Marianne's insistence that Mum wouldn't only listen, she'd understand. "Concerned she won't hear a word being said."

"I know it doesn't always feel like it." Leo reached out and put a hand on my arm. "But I am on your side."

I nodded. "I know. I just sometimes wish you'd–"

"Yoo hoo!"

Leo and I sat up straight, gathering ourselves at the sound of Mum's voice.

"You sure you're ready for this?" Leo said. "Because if you're not…"

Again, I nodded.

"It's only me!"

I took a deep breath as Mum's dulcet tones made a part of me wish I'd ignored Marianne's advice.

Having let herself into the house through the front door, Mum stepped out into the garden from the kitchen. She smiled at the sight of us. "And how are you two this morning?"

I hadn't been face to face with Mum since our evening with Bill and Grace at the restaurant. "Okay," I said. "Considering your antics the last time I saw you."

Mum's face fell. "About that night. Please, let me start by saying I'm sorry."

"Really?"

Mum might have looked sincere, but there was no guarantee of that being the case. I indicated an empty chair and she joined us at the table.

"Yes, really." She hung her bag on the back of her seat and sat down.

"Drink?" Leo asked, gesturing to the cafetière.

"Oooh, please."

While Leo headed inside, only to reappear with another cup, Mum continued with her apology. "I don't know why I behaved the way I did. It was very disrespectful. To you two and to Grace."

"You got that right," I said, although I had to admit that on the night in question Grace had been equally as bad.

"Grace's faith is obviously very important to her and because of that, of course, she's going to want you to marry in the eyes of God."

Mum's comments threw me and as Leo and I exchanged a look, I could see he was as surprised as I was to hear Mum being so understanding. She had never been one to really admit fault and Leo and I both knew her words couldn't have come easy.

"Apology accepted," I said. I steeled myself to continue. "But there are some other things I'd like to talk about, Mum."

"Which is why..." Mum said, putting a hand up to interrupt me.

My back stiffened, as I wondered why Mum couldn't simply say she was sorry and leave it at that.

"Patricia," Leo said, his tone firm but fair. "Tess is trying to speak."

"Which is why," Mum repeated. "I've decided to honour Grace's beliefs."

"What do you mean?" Feeling panicked, I envisaged Mum on the phone to Gregbrook Manor cancelling our wedding in favour of a church ceremony. The way our upcoming nuptials had gone so far, and having already declined Saint Oswald's, it would be our luck to find Reverend Joseph no longer available. All reverends in the vicinity, for that matter. "What have you done?" I asked, at the same time not wanting to know.

Mum smiled, but as was usual of late, that wasn't a good sign. It offered zero reassurance.

"If Grace wants a member of the cloth to officiate your wedding," Mum said. "Then that's what Grace shall have."

I looked at Leo, who appeared as worried as me.

"Meaning?" I asked, returning my attention to Mum.

"Meaning..." Mum's smile grew. Her eyes went from me to Leo and back again. "That you are both now looking at your very own ordained minister."

My brow furrowed, as I realised it had finally happened. My mother had lost the plot. "Excuse me?" I said, while Leo sat there too stunned for words.

"That's right. I will personally be overseeing your marriage vows."

I stared at Mum in disbelief, questioning how that was remotely possible.

"Just so you know, I can also perform baptisms, funerals,

house blessings, baby naming, and a number of other ceremonies, all of which will be outlined when my official documents and certification come through. I even get a badge. Not any old badge, mind. A clergy badge." Mum giggled. "It's surprising what you can do over the internet these days."

Mum had done some ridiculous things in the run-up to our wedding, but getting herself ordained beat them all. I shook my head and threw myself back in my seat. "Incredible."

"Isn't it?" Mum said, not for the first time completely missing my tone.

"Firstly," I said. "I don't know what websites you've been looking at, but it takes a lot more than a Google search and some random sign-up to become a bona fide registrar here in the UK. So, your certificates count for nothing."

"But–"

"And secondly," I said. Deciding it was my turn to interrupt, I leaned forward. "You simply can't help yourself, can you?"

Mum looked back at me confused.

"I mean, first we had Wendy, the wedding planner, to contend with, then we had the wedding dress to beat all wedding dresses." Months of frustration rose to the fore. "Then we had Gregbrook Manor because you didn't want small and intimate, you wanted big."

Leo put a hand on my forearm. "Go easy, Tess."

"Easy? After everything she's done? I don't think so." I shrugged his palm away, determined to finish what I'd started.

"I don't understand," Mum said, her smile gone.

"Yes, Mum, you do."

"But I thought you'd be pleased."

"Pleased?" I let out a mocking laugh. "Initially, I put everything down to your fixation with Louise Patterson's big extravaganza. Now I realise the poor girl has nothing to do with anything, because as usual it's all about you. You're just using the two of us…" I indicated me and Leo. "…to make up for the fact that you didn't have your own dream wedding."

Mum's brow furrowed. "Tess, what are you talking about?"

"Well, you can have it. You and Dad can stand in front of all those people that none of us have seen in years and say I do. Because I'm not playing this game anymore."

"What game?"

I stared at Mum. "I found the price tag."

"What price tag?"

"The one on the inside of your wedding gown. You know, the so-called heirloom that you never actually wore?"

"That doesn't mean your father and I aren't–"

"Don't lie to me, Mum." I couldn't believe she thought I was that stupid.

"Tess, I'm not lying. Me and your dad are most definitely married." She picked up her handbag, found her purse and began rifling through it. Pulling out a photo, she handed it to me. "That's me and your father. On our wedding day."

I stared at the snapshot. With no Princess Diana dress in sight, Mum wore a cream skirt and jacket, while Dad had on navy trousers, white shirt, and a tie. They stood smiling, with their arms linked.

"Don't get me wrong. It might not have been what I dreamt about as a young girl growing up, but it was good enough for us. As for your wedding, I wanted more for the both of you. A proper celebration."

"So where did the wedding gown come from?" I asked.

"I bought it to wear that day." Mum indicated the picture. "But everyone said I'd look daft walking into the registry office in an all-singing all-dancing dress. Which is why I wore the cream suit instead."

"So why lie about it?" I glared at Mum, before waving my hand, dismissive. "In fact, don't answer that, I don't care what your reasons are. You're just a bully. Not only with me, but with everyone."

"Come on, Tess," Leo said. "That's a bit harsh, isn't it?"

I turned to him. "How can you keep being so understanding? Not only has she manipulated everything about our wedding, Leo, Dad can't share his new-found hobby with the rest of his family because of her. After all, being married to a trainspotter is far too embarrassing."

I looked at Mum. "You know what? Forget it. I'm done."

"Tess, you don't…" Mum said.

"What? I don't mean it?"

"Tess?" Leo looked at me, confused. "What are you saying?"

"You need to leave," I said to my mother.

"But…"

"Please, Tess," Leo said. "We need to talk about this."

I couldn't believe what I was hearing. What did he think I'd been trying to do?

"Tess…?"

Ignoring Leo's protests, I sat arms folded, waiting for Mum to get up from her seat. However, with no movement forthcoming, it seemed I'd no choice but to rise to my feet instead. "Looks like I'm the one who's going then, doesn't it?"

CHAPTER 51

assing through the house, I grabbed my keys and bag, before storming out to the car. However, with no idea where I was going, as soon as I climbed into the vehicle, I regretted it. I started the engine regardless and, chewing on the inside of my cheek, considered heading to Sal's. But while my sister understood how frustrating Mum could be, I could already hear her laughter over Mum's ordination. She and Ryan would, without doubt, find Mum's latest stunt funny, rather than see it as the self-centred action it was.

I pictured Mum's smug expression and knowing she hadn't hit the internet out of respect for Grace's faith like she claimed, I scowled. Having spent a full evening competing with Leo's mother, Mum had done it out of one-upmanship. Pure and simple. I felt angry. Infuriated with Mum for ruining everything about my wedding. Plus, I was mad at myself for not being more forceful with her from the beginning. I sighed, knowing that in my resentment I'd also hurt Leo. When I'd lashed out and said I was done, my sole intention had been to upset Mum, not him, and I hated myself for not having thought before I spoke.

I wished I could head south to Cornwall or north to Scotland.

But with Chloe's pregnancy and Abbey's renovations, even though they'd welcome me with open arms, I knew it wouldn't be fair. They had enough to contend with without me and my woes.

Needing to get out of there regardless, I slammed my foot down on the clutch, I grabbed the gearstick, and rammed it forward. The resulting crunching and grinding as it refused to do as I wanted only increased my frustration. I tried again but the noise continued, forcing me to repeat the process for a third time.

I jumped as my door suddenly opened.

Leo stood beside me. "Move over. You're in no state to drive."

Though annoyed at the intrusion, I had to admit he was right. I was way too incensed to be behind the wheel and forced to inch over into the passenger seat, I frowned as I reached for my seat belt. "Come on then," I said, as Leo prepared to set off. "Let's go."

Pulling away, we drove in silence, with me peering out of the side window and Leo staring at the road ahead. Watching the countryside go by, I wanted to say something. But as had kept happening of late, I tried and failed to come up with the right words.

Stealing glances at Leo every now and then, I wondered what was running through his mind. I hated the fact neither of us knew what the other was truly thinking. With our wedding only weeks from then, that was no way for us to start our married life.

At last, Leo flicked on the car indicator and pulled into a lay-by. Bringing the car to a standstill, he switched off the engine and twisted round in his seat to face me. He sighed. "Did you mean what you said? About being done?"

I shrugged, feeling at a loss thanks to the premarital mess we were in. "Yes and no."

"Which makes no sense whatsoever," Leo said.

"Nothing's as I imagined and there's no controlling Mum. As soon as I get my head around one issue, up pops something else to contend with. She's turned the whole thing into a circus. And then there's you." I paused to calm myself. "I suppose I'm confused, Leo. One minute you insist I'm overreacting and tell me Mum's just excited and her heart's in the right place. In the next, you're telling me you're on my side, as if you understand where I'm coming from."

"I agree."

I looked at him surprised. "You do?"

Leo nodded. "Because I think both of those things. No matter what we say, Patricia was always going to go big or go home with this wedding. It's in her nature. She also wants you to have the wedding you deserve. You know your mum. She isn't the type to shower you with affection. And the mood boards, the dress, all the things you listed earlier, are her way of showing you she cares. As for me, none of what your mum's done offends me. If anything, I find her antics funny because they're so over the top. But I also want you to have the wedding you want. What I *don't* want is you looking back with any regrets."

I took a deep breath and no longer able to look at Leo direct, kept my eyes down. "I don't think I can go through with it, Leo. Not the way things are."

Leo sighed. "Me neither."

My head shot up. Whatever I'd expected him to say, it wasn't that. "Really?"

Leo stared at me with such an intenseness that the thought of what he might say next frightened me.

Tears threatened my eyes. "So where does this leave us?"

"Tess, I love you with all my heart and want nothing more than for us to be man and wife."

But?

Leo might not have said that. However, the word hung in the air between us.

Leo took a deep breath and slowly exhaled. "I think you're right. The wedding we planned is nothing like the one we seem to be getting and believe it or not, I don't want to say my vows in front of a room full of strangers either. I think we should pay your mum back any money she'll lose and..."

"Call it off?"

As Leo nodded, my heart felt like it was breaking and despite willing them not to, my tears began to fall.

CHAPTER 52

A RANDOM TUESDAY IN AUGUST

I laid in bed staring at the ceiling, with images of Mum's perfect wedding running through my mind. From waking up in a king-size bed, in a luxury suite in Gregbrook Manor, to a champagne breakfast of pastries, fresh fruits, bacon and eggs, and most importantly, fizz. My mouth watered just thinking about it.

I saw myself waiting for a hairdresser and make-up artist to arrive, ready to set up their stalls and turn me into a bridal princess, while Mum, in an adjacent room, fussed over arrangements and Dad rehearsed his father-of-the-bride speech. Sal and Ryan were discussing which items to snaffle from their quarters – shampoo, conditioner, slippers. And smiling to myself, I saw them squeezing white towelling dressing gowns into their travel bags.

Ignoring her thieving parents, India practised her walk, because it was her duty to show off a fellow dressmaker's creation. As for Grace and Bill, in my mind's eye they were driving down from the Lake District with Nial and Victoria.

Turning onto my side, I tucked my hands under my cheek. A part of me felt sad that none of it was to be. Not for myself, but for Mum. Hindsight was a wonderful thing, and I no longer doubted that she thought she'd had my and Leo's best interests at heart. However, at the time, when her antics had become increasingly too much, she'd left us no choice but to cancel the whole thing. Picturing her desperateness when we told her the wedding was off, I sighed.

"But... but... You can't," she'd said, lost for words.

No matter how we explained, she couldn't seem to comprehend our reasoning; I'd never seen her so distressed. I was just glad Dad was there to pick up the pieces after we'd gone.

Our decision may have affected Mum the worst, but everyone else had expressed their own kind of disappointment. Acknowledging the sadness in Dad's eyes, I hadn't realised how much he'd looked forward to walking me down the aisle. Taking that honour away made me feel like the worst daughter on the planet. India hadn't only sulked, she'd turned her displeasure on Leo and stormed away from him, which was a first. Then there was Sal and Ryan. Although understanding, they hadn't just looked forward to giving Leo a proper welcome into the family, they'd had their sights on a good knees-up.

Yet again telling myself the Cavendishes would get over it, I thought it no wonder I'd avoided contact with them for weeks on end. As for Abbey and Chloe, I hadn't said anything to them at all. But with one opening a new gallery and the other soon to have a baby, I was delaying the inevitable for as long as I could.

"Good morning," Leo said, appearing in the doorway. He wore a gentle smile and much to my surprise carried a tray.

"What's all this?" I asked, hoisting myself up into a seated position.

"I thought you might like breakfast in bed."

"Thank you," I said appreciating his thoughtfulness.

Leo placed the tray on my lap. "Voila!"

As good as any start to the day that Gregbrook Manor could provide, I picked up the cup of coffee and taking a sip, savoured the taste. "Wonderful." Turning my attention to the toasted bagels and marmalade, I dived straight in.

"How are you feeling?" Leo asked. He sat down on the edge of the bed next to me.

My eyes were drawn to the wedding dress that hung off my wardrobe door. "Happy yet sad, if that makes sense?"

He followed my gaze. "It does." Leo turned back to me, his expression one of concern. "Any regrets?"

I shook my head. "Not really." I carried on eating. "You?"

"Nope." He leaned in and kissed the top of my head. "We made the right decision."

I nodded. "I think so too."

He raised his eyebrows and smiled again. "I've run you a bath."

"Oooh, I am getting special treatment."

Leo chuckled. "If I can't spoil you on a day like today, then when can I?"

CHAPTER 53

*H*aving parked up the car, Leo and I walked hand in hand through town. The weather gods were smiling down on us and the sun shone in celebration. Strangers smiled our way as we strode along and not used to such scrutiny, my cheeks flushed red with embarrassment. Some wished us all the best. Others simply cooed.

"Good luck," one elderly lady made a point of saying.

"Don't do it," one chap called out.

At last, reaching our destination, Leo and I came to a stop. I didn't think I'd ever felt so nervous as we looked up at the historic limestone building. Flower boxes filled with violet, yellow, and orange blooms adorned the tall sash window ledges, and ornate chiselled carvings framed the ginormous wooden double doors. The Town Hall's edifice wasn't just imposing, it proudly showed off its importance. Butterflies played havoc in my tummy as the two of us prepared to climb the steps that paved the way to the entrance.

"I can't believe we're doing this," I said.

Leo squeezed my hand. "Not a bad way to spend a random Tuesday afternoon though, eh?"

I thought back to all those months earlier when Leo had suggested we get married on exactly that kind of day. Then, I might have found his proposition romantic, but I never thought we'd end up doing it. I smiled. "Not bad at all."

I took a deep breath. "How do I look?" I'd spent the whole morning pampering and preening; luxuriating in the hot bath Leo had run for me and spending far longer than necessary styling my hair into rich side-swept curls. I might not have worn a lot of make-up, but perfecting what I had put on took ages.

Never one to dress up, by the time I slipped into Marianne's creation and the blush pink Vivienne Westwood shoes, I looked and felt like a brand-new person. "My lipstick hasn't smudged, or mascara run, has it?" I held the twined wildflower bouquet that Leo had made for me out to one side, so he could assess my whole ensemble uninterrupted.

"You look beautiful," he said, his intense stare making my heart race.

I took in Leo's attire. Going for smart yet casual, he wore suit trousers and a waistcoat. His tie had been fashioned into a loose knot, and his shirt sleeves were rolled up to just below his elbows. The man had obviously paid attention to our early conversations, because he looked exactly how I'd described following my Indian summer dream.

"Ready?" he asked.

I nodded. "Ready."

As we made our way up to the registry office doors, I couldn't deny our actions felt bittersweet. On the one hand, after months of setbacks and unnecessary stresses and strains, I couldn't believe we were finally getting married. On the other, I wanted our families and Otis there to celebrate with us. Putting my sadness over absent friends and family to one side, I told myself the situation was what it was.

Leo paused at the entrance. "After you." With an exaggerated flourish of his hand, he bowed and stood aside.

"Why thank you," I replied and stepped into the building.

"Surprise!"

Shocked not only by the sound but also the people before me, my eyes widened. I put my hand up to my chest and I tried to speak, but felt too stunned for words.

"You didn't think we'd let you get wed without us, did you?" Sal said, laughing. She indicated her gorgeous matron of honour dress and gave a little curtsey. "What do you think?"

"Stunning," I replied, at last finding my voice.

I turned to Leo, unable to believe he'd not only arranged this, but also managed to keep things a secret. "How?" I stood with a big smile on my face, recovering from the shock. "When?"

"I knew, deep down, you'd want everyone here. No wedding day regrets, remember?"

"I love you," I said, reaching up to kiss him.

"Save it for after the ceremony," Ryan called out, making everyone laugh.

As tears filled my eyes, Bill stepped forward with a checked handkerchief so I could blot away any rogue mascara.

"Thank you," I said, unable to help but smile when Grace approached, dabbing her tears away with an exact replica. Leo's dad had obviously come prepared.

"Be devoted to one another in love. Honour one another above yourselves," Grace said. "Romans, Chapter 12, Verse 10." She smiled. "Follow that advice and you won't go far wrong."

"Cheers, Mum," Leo said, giving her a hug.

Grace admired my dress, before suddenly cocking her head. "Is this…?" She looked over to India and Sal. "Are they…?"

"Yes," I replied. "And all thanks to my friend over there." I pointed to Marianne who no one could miss thanks to her outfit's exuberant clash of colour and print. "I couldn't wear Mum's wedding gown and not yours and vice versa, so to make sure I didn't have to choose, she used the fabric from both to create all our dresses." I crinkled my face. "You're not mad, are you?"

Grace let out a laugh. "Mad? I think it's ingenious."

"And I, for one, think you all look wonderful," Bill said. He took a deep breath. "I can't tell you how happy we are to be here."

"I'm happy you're here too," I said.

"And me," Leo added.

Glancing around, I thought my heart might burst as I took in our guests.

India owned her chiffon bridesmaid dress and after a month of not seeing her, I was pleased to find her fringe had grown somewhat. She strode first one way, and then the other, as if practising her modelling skills, leaving me hoping she wouldn't be too disappointed when she realised her registry office catwalk was lacking.

"You look perfect," Marianne mouthed. She beamed proudly as she linked arms with her husband. It was the first time I'd seen Hugo in person and watching him animatedly chat and point out the space's original cornicing and ceiling rose, he seemed as passionate about buildings as he was locomotives.

Any other guest and I might have raised an eyebrow at Hugo's peaked train driver cap. But having seen his and Dad's enthusiasm over a 201 Thumper, I found the addition quite sweet. Glad of his and Marianne's presence, I felt pleased that Leo had thought to invite them.

My eyes settled on Mum and Dad. I wasn't surprised to see that Mum was the only female guest to wear a hat and I had to admit her huge-brimmed, navy, organza affair with massive bow at the side looked astonishingly good. Mum clocked my interest and as she gave me a sheepish smile a sob suddenly escaped my lips. Before I could stop myself, I raced over and threw my arms around her. Holding her tight for a moment, I, at last, let go.

"I'm so sorry," Mum said, her eyes welling up. "I just wanted…"

"I know." I thought about how angry I'd been when Mum and I last met, recalling the venom with which I'd spoken to her. "And I'm sorry too."

"I can't believe my baby's getting married," Dad said, in danger of crying along with his wife and daughter.

"I can't believe what you've done to my dress," Mum said. "Don't think I haven't noticed."

I held my breath for a moment and as I waited for her to continue, I couldn't tell which way her comments would go.

"It's exquisite, Tess. Absolutely beautiful." She turned to look at my sister and niece. "As are…" Suddenly lost for words, Mum's tears didn't simply well, they flowed.

"You really think so?" I asked.

Mum nodded.

I'd never seen her so emotional that she couldn't speak before and while I chuckled through my tears, relieved to hear she was happy with what I'd done, Bill stepped forward with handkerchiefs for my parents too.

"I know this isn't Gregbrook Manor, Mum, but…"

Mum tried to pull herself together. "About that," she said, mid snivel. "There's something I should probably tell…"

Our attention was diverted when a voice interrupted us before Mum could finish.

"Are we ready to go in?" the registrar said.

CHAPTER 54

*A*ppearing at my side, Leo took my hand. "Looks like this is it."

I had to take deep breaths as we all followed the registrar into the ceremony room. As everyone took a seat and Leo and I took our places at the top of the aisle, it was all eyes on us and not one to relish being the centre of events, nervousness threatened to overwhelm me.

Leo gave me a wink. "You'll be fine," he said, whispering in my ear.

Feeling a tad warm, I nodded. "I just hope I don't faint."

With guests settled in their seats, the registrar again began to speak, but her words passed me by in a blur. My mind kept wandering back to everything that had happened those last months. Thanks to the good, the bad, and the ugly, Leo and I had had quite a journey. The registrar's voice suddenly got louder, jolting me to attention.

"You are here to witness the joining in marriage of Leo McDermot and Tessa Cavendish," she said. "If any person present knows of any lawful impediment why these two people may not be joined in marriage, he or she should declare it now."

Standing there, while I didn't anticipate a member of any first wives club making an appearance, I held on to lungs full of air, half expecting Ryan to blurt something out for effect. However, Sal was obviously keeping her man in check because the room stayed silent and finally, I allowed myself to exhale.

"Could I ask you both to hold hands," the registrar said to Leo and me.

As we turned to face each other, the registrar continued to speak. I heard words like matrimony, solemn, and binding. But as I continued to focus on my breathing, I was too busy trying to stop my hands shaking to pay proper heed.

Leo squeezed my palms and being just what I needed, his reassurance calmed my nerves enough for me to finally listen.

"These vows which unite you as husband and wife, constitute a formal and public pledge of your love for one another," the registrar said.

Oh, Lordy, I thought, realising the time had come for us to speak.

She turned her attention solely to Leo. "Are you, Leo McDermot, free to lawfully marry Tessa Cavendish."

"I am," Leo replied, his voice loud and clear.

The registrar turned to me. "Are you, Tessa Cavendish, free to lawfully marry Leo McDermot."

I nodded.

Smiling at me, the registrar indicated I needed to say it out loud, which generated a few laughs amongst our audience.

"Sorry." I felt myself blush. "Yes. I am," I replied, my voice shaky.

The registrar looked to our guests and after explaining what was to happen next, asked everyone to stand.

Neither Leo nor I took our eyes off one another as sentence by sentence, we each called upon everyone present to witness us becoming man and wife. Leo silently encouraged me every step of the way and as we said our vows and exchanged rings, despite the *oohs* and *aahs* from the rest of our wedding party, such was our concentration, it was as if Leo and I were the only two people in the room. The whole ceremony seemed to go by in no time.

"It therefore gives me the greatest honour and privilege," the registrar said. "To announce that you are now husband and wife."

Our whole wedding party whooped and cheered in celebration.

"You may now kiss the bride," the registrar said.

As he stepped towards me and put his hands on my hips, Leo and I couldn't help but giggle. But as he leaned in and his lips met mine, we were soon lost in our first wonderful embrace as a married couple.

More cheers erupted amongst our guests, and bringing our kiss to an end, Leo rested his forehead on mine. "We did it," he said.

Tears welled in my eyes. "I know."

"Ladies and gentlemen," the registrar said. "I give you Mr and Mrs McDermot."

Leo took my hand and together, wearing the biggest of smiles, we turned to face our guests.

EPILOGUE

SECOND SATURDAY IN SEPTEMBER

ollowing that random Tuesday in August, Leo and I escaped to Northumbria for a few glorious days. Having tried to explain herself before our wedding, only to be interrupted, Mum had left it until we got back to tell us that she hadn't cancelled Gregbrook Manor. Not only had she been too embarrassed to inform everyone that the ceremony was off, she'd secretly hoped that I'd change my mind and go through with it. Even as she explained, it was evident she continued to consider that a possibility.

Sat around the dinner table at our Cavendish family get-together, my look had gone from Mum and Dad, to Sal, Ryan and India, before finally settling on Leo. Our original wedding had been so much fun, I wasn't surprised to find each of them staring back at me in eager anticipation.

"Shall we?" Leo had said, clearly excited by the prospect.

"I think our dresses deserve another outing," Sal said.

"Me too," India said.

"See it as a big party to celebrate," Ryan said.

Sitting there in his station master's uniform, Dad smiled. "And I'd love the chance to walk you down the aisle."

"Instead of another wedding you could call it a blessing," Mum said. "Please?"

With each of them making a good point and me still on a newly-wed high, I supposed it no wonder I found myself having a wonderful stay at Gregbrook Manor.

The venue's champagne breakfast was as good as I'd imagined, although standing there with Dad and India, waiting for our cue, I wished I hadn't availed myself of quite so many pastries.

"You okay, love?" Dad asked, looking handsome and dashing in his grey morning suit.

I took a deep breath. "I don't know why I'm so nervous. It's not like I haven't done this before."

"I can't wait to get in there," India said, her words coming as no surprise.

I smiled at her, wishing I had some of her confidence. While Sal had been happy to sit amongst the guests, no way was India being deprived of her moment, so it wasn't like she didn't have any to spare. Watching her take a peek into the orangery, I recalled India's short-lived days as a fashion model. With her once-butchered fringe now overgrown and clipped to the side, it was as if the incident with the scissors had never happened.

"This is so exciting," she said.

A member of Gregbrook's staff stepped forward and with a nod, informed us that it was time to start.

Dad and I steeled ourselves, while India fussed about straightening her dress.

"How do I look?" I asked.

"Like a beautiful princess." Dad glanced at India. "You both do," he said, his face full of pride. He raised his eyebrows. "Ready to go?"

While my niece gave him an emphatic yes, I inhaled again. "As I'll ever be."

The orangery doors opened, just as the wedding chorus

kicked in. Dad smiled as he took my arm, and the three of us stepped forward to walk down the aisle.

As we made our entrance, I didn't know who gasped the loudest. The huge wedding party that Mum had invited, or me? I was shocked at how many people were willing to attend the wedding of someone they hadn't seen for years and hardly knew. Try as I might, I struggled to spot proper family and friends amongst everyone. "This is madness," I said to Dad, through a fixed smile.

"Enjoy the moment," Dad replied, soaking up the attention. "That's what I'm doing."

As my eyes continued to search, I, at last, saw Abbey and a heavily pregnant Chloe. Tissues to hand, they beamed my way. I was so pleased they'd made it and I couldn't wait to properly catch up with them after the service.

"Aunty Tess!" Ruby called out. Climbing up on her chair, she frantically waved, causing a ripple of laughter amongst all the guests.

"Hello, sweetheart," I replied, my voice shaking.

It was the sight of Leo waiting for me that kept me moving forward. Although he wasn't the only one to melt my heart; wearing a shirt collar and bright red tie, Otis did too. I was clearly the odd one out, because, like Dad and India, Leo appeared to be relishing every second of the proceedings. As was Mum, I also noted.

Trying not to laugh, I took in her serious demeanour as Dad and I, at last, came to a standstill. Holding a book in her hand, she wore a straight face, a long black vestment, and a stole embellished with a dove on one side and a pair of wedding rings on the other.

Looking every inch the ordained minister, Mum looked out on the congregation. "We are gathered here today…"

THE END

ACKNOWLEDGEMENTS

I'd like to start by thanking everyone at Bloodhound Books. Especially Betsy and Fred for your unwavering support in my writing journey. Thanks go to my editor Morgen. Every time we work together, I learn something new. I'd like to thank Tara for all the work you do at every stage of the publication process. My heartfelt appreciation goes out to Hannah, Shirley and Maria. You really are a fabulous team to work with.

A special thank you goes out to cake maker extraordinaire Fiona King. Not only have you made me some wonderful book launch cakes, without your input Tess would have probably ended up with a simple vanilla sponge to celebrate her big day with. Not that there's anything wrong with a vanilla sponge. Just ask my waistline!

I'm not known for my fashion knowledge and didn't know where to start when trying to come up with a suitable name for a world-famous designer. So, an equally special thank you goes out to my Facebook followers who stepped into the breach. You gave me some brilliant suggestions and thanks to Carly Thomas and Yvonne Bastian in particular, Zane Rafferty was born. Still Zane Rafferty related, I'd like to thank Janie Atkins too. Your knowledge of the Dutch artist Piet Mondrian helped me form a picture as to the inspiration behind Zane's creations.

Finally, and I know I say this every time I release a book, I really would like to thank all my readers. Without you I wouldn't be doing the job I love. I hope my stories continue to make you laugh and, at times, cry. And that they take you to the same happy place they take me as I write them.

Happy reading, everyone!

Suzie x

A NOTE FROM THE PUBLISHER

Thank you for reading this book. If you enjoyed it please do consider leaving a review on Amazon to help others find it too.

We hate typos. All of our books have been rigorously edited and proofread, but sometimes mistakes do slip through. If you have spotted a typo, please do let us know and we can get it amended within hours.

info@bloodhoundbooks.com

Printed in Great Britain
by Amazon

84691412R00150